CARTBOY GOES TO CAMP

Also by L. A. Campbell

Cartboy and the Time Capsule

CARTBOY GOES TO CAMP

L. A. Campbell

STARSCAPE

A Tom Doherty Associates Book
New York

CARTBOY GOES TO CAMP

Copyright © 2014 by L. A. Campbell

A Starscape Book
Published by Tom Doherty Associates, LLC
175 Fifth Avenue
New York, NY 10010

www.tor-forge.com

The Library of Congress Cataloging-in-Publication Data is available upon request.

ISBN 978-0-7653-3327-8 (paper over board)
ISBN 978-1-4668-0202-5 (e-book)

Starscape books may be purchased for educational, business, or promotional use. For information on bulk purchases, please contact Macmillan Corporate and Premium Sales Department at 1-800-221-7945, extension 5442, or write specialmarkets@macmillan.com.

First Edition: June 2014

0 9 8 7 6 5 4 3 2 1

To Beau and Charlie

CARTBOY GOES TO CAMP

Dear Person/Alien Who Lives Way in the Future:

Hello. Greetings. Zimnet Snerg.

It's me, Hal.

The first thing I want to say is: sorry to bug you again. I'm sure you have better things to do. Like play soccer on Jupiter. Or visit your robot cousins on Mars.

But based on what happened today, I had to talk to *someone*. And I figured the best someone was you. Especially since I wrote to you all last year in my time capsule journal for Mr. Tupkin's history class. (Yes, I am still recovering.)

Human hand.

Human hand after writing a
journal for the entire sixth grade.

I'm also hoping you have the means (a real
working time machine) and the power (alien awe-
someness) to beam me out of here.

Based on what happened today with my dad,
I'm more desperate now than *ever.*

It all started when my best friend, Arnie
Giannelli, came over to my house. It was the first
day of summer, and we had big plans to get to
Level 15 of *RavenCave.* We didn't want to waste a

minute. So we sat down in the room I share with my twin sisters, Bea and Perrie, and turned on the computer.

We had just started playing, when my dad's voice came from the living room. "Hal, I need to speak with you," he said.

As soon as I heard him, I did what any sensible kid would do. Covered my ears with a stuffed animal. This time I used Flatso the Hippo, who I found in Bea's crib.

I wrapped Flatso over my head and pressed down hard. Whatever my dad had to say, I was pretty sure I didn't want to hear it. Partly because of the suspicious-looking piece of paper I saw in his pocket right before Arnie came over.

And partly because summer was finally here. And, like I mentioned before, Arnie and I had important goals to achieve:

Noon:	Wake up
12:30:	Eat doughnuts
12:40–3:00:	Get to Level 15

As it turns out, holding a stuffed animal over my ears was about as useful as holding a handful of air.

"Hal. Get in here now."

I put Flatso back in the crib and dragged myself into the living room. My dad was sitting on our worn-out couch wearing one of his Revolutionary War uniforms. He had just come from reenacting a battle down by the town tennis courts, so he had a rip in his jacket. And about five missing buttons.

"Rough skirmish today, Dad?"

"We were badly outnumbered by the British. I took a bayonet to the ribs."

Blood my dad uses when he reenacts a battle.
Tastes great on a burger.

"Sorry to hear you lost the fight, Dad. Better luck next time!" I started to make a beeline back to *RavenCave,* but I didn't get far.

"Sit," said my dad.

I sat. I've learned that when my dad says to sit, you should probably do it. Unless you want to end up raking leaves for five hours on a Saturday.

I could tell he was going to get down to the real reason he wanted to talk to me. And that it was much bigger than telling me about a battle he just lost.

My dad shifted around for what felt like nine hours—then finally his lips started to move. "Hal, now that you're twelve, I think it's time for you to look at summer differently. To expand your horizons. It's time for you to get out of Stowfield, Pennsylvania."

"You mean, like, go to Grampa Janson's for a couple of days?"

That I could handle. Grampa Janson has a giant gumball machine in his basement, and you don't even have to use a quarter to get one out.

"No, not Grampa Janson's," said my dad. "I'm talking about *really* getting away from Stowfield. Having an . . . experience. Your mom and I have decided to send you to sleepaway camp. For two weeks."

Sleepaway camp?

The only summer camp I'd ever been to was the Tiny Wishes Day Camp near the bowling alley downtown. Tiny Wishes was made up of a diverse mix of children: 99 percent little kids, and me. I'm pretty sure I was the only person in the pool who didn't wear swim diapers.

Percentage of pee a swim diaper prevents
from going in a pool: 0

I looked my dad in the eyes. "You mean you and Mom are sending me to a real summer camp? One that has cabins and sports?"

"Exactly."

"Nature?"

"Uh-huh."

"Kids over the age of four?"

"Yes."

"Sounds like I'll be needing a skateboard and a tennis racket and some new basketball sneakers! I think they're having a sale over at Denby's. I'll meet you in the car—"

"Hold on."

"Okay, maybe just the skateboard. And the sneakers—"

"Hal. You won't be needing any of that fancy new stuff. This is a special camp. A different kind of place."

Okay, I thought, that could still mean it wasn't bad. There would probably still be lots of s'mores.

A Guide to How a Human Feels After Eating S'mores

🍪🍪🍪	Not too bad.
🍪🍪🍪🍪	Pretty sick.
🍪🍪🍪🍪🍪	Seriously want to barf.
🍪🍪🍪🍪🍪	Vomiting out your eyeballs.
🍪🍪🍪🍪🍪🍪	Want to die.

Just as I was picturing the marshmallow goo melting all over my tongue, my dad slid a piece of paper toward me. I picked it up and saw it was a brochure for a place called Camp Jamestown. Judging by the trees and the pond on the cover, it didn't seem so bad.

Then I took a closer look.

Standing by a log cabin was an old guy with a beard that came to a sharp point at the end.

Guys who like   Guitarists for
colonial times.   Ultradeath.

"Um. Exactly what kind of camp is this, Dad?"

"The best camp in the world, that's what kind. You get to live like a real pioneer!" My dad started flipping through the brochure, pointing to pictures of pine trees and cabins and outhouses. "Hardly anything has changed at Camp Jamestown since the 1600s! It's woodsy and rustic and there's wildlife everywhere. One time, I even saw a bear!"

"Dad," I said, wiping a gob of sweat off my fore-head. "I *so* appreciate your kind offer. But, um, for the sake of our family and the meager-to-nonexistent funds you earn from fixing appliances for a living, I will generously decline. For you and Mom and the twins, I'll stay home."

With that, I attempted to walk away.

"Nice try, mister. Get back here."

I turned back, and that's when I noticed the humongous bag on the floor. It was open on one end, and a spider the size of a *hockey puck* crawled out.

Bugs That Like to Live Inside Your Stuff
More than Nature

Ant

Spider

Crunchy biting bug

Scary ugly bug

Bug your mom
finds in the rice and
makes you eat anyway

Freaky roach
thing

"Shoo," said my dad, waving away the spider. "Guess he couldn't resist making a home out of this beauty."

The "beauty" was a mold-covered, army-green duffel bag my dad had somehow dragged up from the basement.

"This was my pack when I went to Camp Jamestown. And before that, it was Grampa Janson's army bag. Check it out. It's filled with supplies!"

My dad reached inside the bag and started pulling stuff out. "Ah yes, the old canteen. My trusty shovel. Bow and arrow. Ax. Sewing kit. Oooh! My yarn spindle!"

Sewing kit? Yarn spindle?

"These precious heirlooms helped me win Pioneer Day. Look at the beadwork on this fabric. I made a bald eagle. Very sacred to the Powhatan Indians. But you'll learn all about that. Starting tomorrow."

"T-tomorrow?"

"The bus leaves first thing in the morning."

My dad went over the checklist of stuff every camper was supposed to bring. "Good thing I saved almost everything on the list," he said. "No frivolous shopping for us!"

I stared at all the "precious heirlooms" and couldn't help but think, Here we go again.

It wasn't enough that my dad made me carry my books to school in an old-lady cart for most of sixth grade. Now he was going to make me be the weird kid at camp too. The kid with the stuff his dad thinks is "priceless." But everyone else knows is junk. Even the sleeping bag was full of holes.

"Dad," I said as a last-ditch effort. "This duffel bag is way too heavy for me. Remember what you said about bad backs running in the family . . ."

"I've already thought of that. You can carry the bag in your cart!"

The reason everyone calls me Cartboy.

I looked down at the duffel bag by my feet and couldn't help but wish there were something else inside it.

Not a shovel. Or a bow and arrow. Or a yarn spindle.

But a molecular modifier. Like the kind I saw on the TV show *Gadgets of the Future*. It transports you anywhere in time you want to go.

They said everyone in the distant future will have one. Which brings me to the question I always seem to be asking you.

You don't have one handy, do you?

Sleeping Bag Issue

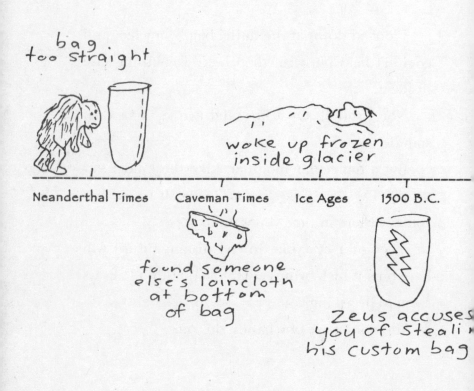

bag
too straight

woke up frozen
inside glacier

Neanderthal Times   Caveman Times   Ice Ages   1500 B.C.

found someone
else's loincloth
at bottom
of bag

Zeus accuses
you of stealin
his custom bag

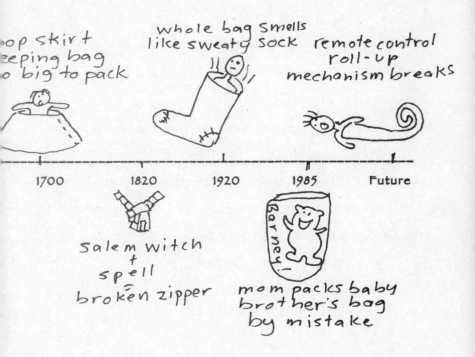

hroughout The Ages

hoop skirt
sleeping bag
too big to pack

whole bag smells
like sweaty sock

remote control
roll-up
mechanism breaks

1700   1820   1920   1985   Future

Salem witch
+
spell
=
broken zipper

Barney!

mom packs baby
brother's bag
by mistake

The Bus

Dear Future Being Who I'm Praying Is Still
Reading This:

The bus to camp left at eight in the morning. It was
parked outside the Stowfield Historical Society,
about a two-minute drive from our house. I guess
they figured the Historical Society was a good meet-
ing place. Seeing as how we were all headed on a
"journey to the colonial past."

One time the Pittsfield Tigers played the Stowfield Pilgrims in basketball. We lost 56–13.

My whole family drove me to the bus, and when we got there, I thought I better say "so long" right away. Probably best to get it over with, since I'm not a big one for good-byes. That, and I felt like if I waited too long, I'd start blubbering like an idiot.

I turned to give my mom a hug good-bye.

"I packed some extra clothes in the duffel bag for you," she said. "You know, warm stuff, an extra toothbrush, your dinosaur underwear—"

"Mom. I haven't worn those dinosaur underwear in six years!"

"But they're so cute . . ."

I turned to get on the bus, and who was standing right in front of me?

Yep. Arnie. He had come to see me off.

"Good luck, bro. If I get to Level 15 on *Raven-Cave,* I'll give you a call," he said.

"No phones," my dad chimed in.

"I'll e-mail."

"Not allowed," my dad said with a smile.

"I'll write?"

My dad looked at Arnie and nodded yes. "But try to use a quill pen."

Arnie whispered into my ear. "Look on the bright side, Hal. You won't be anywhere near Ryan Horner."

I had to admit Arnie had a point. Ryan Horner was convinced I told Mr. Tupkin he cheated on the history final. Which I didn't. But that didn't stop

Ryan from giving me his famous Sweatpants Wedgie in the locker room on the last day of school.

Injuries Caused by the Sweatpants Wedgie

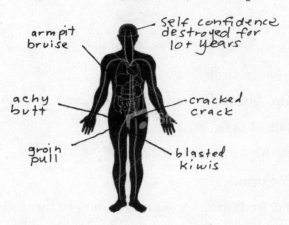

armpit bruise

self confidence destroyed for 10+ years

achy butt

cracked crack

groin pull

blasted kiwis

Suddenly the bus to camp didn't seem so terrible.

"Seven hours to Jamestown, Virginia," said the driver over the loudspeaker. "All aboard."

I waved good-bye to my family, walked on the bus, and grabbed a seat. I was pretty surprised to see the seats were soft and velvety. And there was another bonus—something I don't experience often: real air-conditioning.

The "A/C" at my house.

The bus pulled away, so I sat back and let the cool air blow on my face.

"Ahhh," I said out loud.

"Enjoy it."

I looked up to see a kid standing in the aisle. He was small like me, but his hair stuck straight up. Like he had used a whole bucket of gel on it.

"It's the last blast of cold air you're gonna feel for two weeks." The kid put out his hand. "Vinny Ramirez. Westwood, New Jersey."

"Hal Rifkind."

"You're the one with the old-lady cart? What's up with that?"

"It's a long story."

Unfortunately, Vinny took that as invitation to

sit next to me. "I love stories. Especially history stories. This will be my fourth year at Camp Jamestown."

"You're saying you *willingly* go to this place every summer?"

"I like history. I'm guessing you do too. Since you're here."

"Actually, I was hoping for more of a sporty camp . . ."

I was about to tell Vinny all about this place I heard about called Camp Woodward. It's in Pennsylvania. They have a skateboard park. And a waterslide. You can eat a hamburger every night if you want, and you don't even have to take showers.

But I could tell Vinny wasn't listening. He had pulled a huge *map* out of his backpack and was studying it with an intense look on his face.

"What's that?" I asked.

Vinny looked around the bus, then whispered into my ear. "I'll tell you. But you have to promise not to tell anyone."

He glanced around one more time to make

sure no one was listening. "It's a map of Camp Jamestown," he said. "I drew it myself. To help me find the buried treasure."

Things people usually find where they think a treasure is buried.

I let out a little chuckle. But then I saw that Vinny wasn't kidding.

"I have good reason to believe the treasure was buried a long time ago. Right on camp grounds," he said.

"What is the treasure?" I asked.

"Pearls."

My grandma had some pearls that she sold at a garage sale for four bucks.

Vinny put down the map and looked me in the eyes. "I heard your friend say you almost made it to Level 15 of *RavenCave*. You must be pretty good at hunting for stuff. Do you want to help me find the treasure?"

"Um, *RavenCave* is a video game, Vinny. That's different—"

"Plus we'll both be in the same cabin. Since our last names begin with *R*. That'll make it easier to hunt together."

"I'm not too good at math, Vinny, but even I know that if we share the profits, it'll only be about two dollars each."

"These are real pearls. Pearls the Powhatan Indians traded for food and tools. They could be worth *a lot*. The antiques dealer back home already told me he'd buy them if we found them."

"Thanks, Vinny, but I think I'll pass."

"Suit yourself."

With that, Vinny leaned back and studied his map again. While he sat there reading, I couldn't help but look over his shoulder.

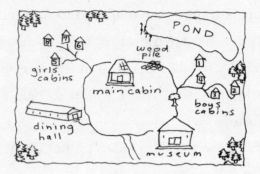

The more I looked at Vinny's map, the more I couldn't help but think the treasure might be real. That helping Vinny hunt for it might be a good thing.

Maybe the treasure would be the solution to all my problems.

I could use the money to buy a motorized scooter to help me carry my books to school. I could finally get rid of my cart. Finally, everyone would stop calling me Cartboy.

I leaned into Vinny's ear. "Okay. I'm in. If we find the treasure, we split it fifty–fifty?"

"Sixty–forty. I did all the research."

"Deal."

I sat there for the rest of the bus ride, thinking about the Ziptuk E300S motorized scooter I was going to get.

The #1 vehicle for transporting books and escaping eighth-grade thugs named Ryan Horner.

I must have been thinking about that scooter a lot, because before I knew it, we were there.

Camp Jamestown. Deep in the woods. Right in the middle of nowhere.

Camp Jamestown

Dear Future Rescuer (I Hope):

We pulled into a clearing in the woods, and about fifty campers and counselors got off the bus. The group was about half girls and half boys, each of us lugging a bag full of gear.

I stood in the clearing with my cart and took a good look around. Right away, three words came to mind.

Not too bad.

Yes, there were crooked old cabins. Outhouses. And a Museum of Colonial Artifacts. And yes, the main cabin near the middle of camp had a *butter churner* on the front porch.

But there were pine trees everywhere. The air smelled fresh and clean. And just past the clearing was a pond lined with lily pads.

Besides, I figured, there had to be *something* modern here. I mean, even though this was a history camp, it was still a camp for *kids*.

Surely there was a kite board or a water trampoline down by the pond. Surely something here had been manufactured in the last twenty years.

The water trampoline. Why kids everywhere pretend they're not homesick.

I looked near the tops of the pine trees for a power line, and across the clearing for flushing toilets. I took a few steps toward the main cabin, where I thought I saw a cell phone through a tiny glass window.

And that's when I heard the sound.

Doo Do Do Looo!

A man holding a dried-out orange gourd walked out of the cabin. I could tell it was the guy from the brochure because of the long pointy beard.

"Welcome, boys, girls, counselors, and history lovers of all kinds!" he said. "I am Mr. Prentice. Thy camp director. And musical gourd player."

You can make anything from a gourd
if you try hard enough.

One look at Mr. Prentice, and any hopes I had for something modern disappeared like a balloon in the wind.

Not only was he playing a *gourd,* but he was also wearing tights and a wool coat that went down to his knees. Underneath the coat was a lacy shirt, like the kind Gramma Janson wears to the opera. He was even wearing those black Pilgrim shoes with the buckles on the sides.

Mr. Prentice put the gourd to his lips and blew hard.

Doo Do Do Looo!

"Gather round, my good people. There's no time liketh the present to discover the past."

Everyone shuffled toward Mr. Prentice, but I, for one, stayed back. That is, until Vinny tugged my arm.

"Let's get up close."

"That's okay, Vinny," I started to say. But Vinny and I got caught up in the crowd, and before we knew it, we were *two feet* in front of Mr. Prentice.

"I'd like to begin your Jamestown experience," he said, "by asking ye a simple question: What is the best way to learn history?"

For reasons I can't begin to understand, he pointed right at me.

"You. Young man. What do you think is the best way to learn history?"

I racked my brain to think of what I learned in Mr. Tupkin's class last year. But when it comes to history stuff, my mind pretty much goes blank.

"Um, flashcards?" I said.

"Try again."

"The Discovery Channel?"

"No."

"YouTube?"

"Christopher Lord of Columbus! What is your name?"

"Hal Rifkind, sir."

"Mr. Rifkind. The best way to learn history is to live it! Every day. And that's exactly what ye shall do here."

Mr. Prentice pulled a small scroll out of his coat and unrolled it. "Now, I'm not going to sugarcoat it. Life at Jamestown in the year 1607 wasn't easy. The settlers suffered hard weather. Severe food shortages. And battles with the Powhatan Indians."

He took a few steps toward us, but his foot got caught on a rock. "*Ow*. And these shoes weren't doing them any favors. But just because this is a history camp doesn't mean we can't do lots of fun and kid-friendly activities!"

Cutting wood
Carving canoes
Beading leather
Bow & arrow hunting
Churning butter
Digging for artifacts

By the time I finished reading Mr. Prentice's scroll,
I was still looking for a kid-friendly activity.

"And the best part," said Mr. Prentice, "is these daily activities will prepare ye for Pioneer Day. A competition on the second-to-last day of camp that includes all the main aspects of pioneer survival. Food, clothing, shelter—"

A girl's hand shot up. "Mr. Prentice," she said. "Will the bow-and-arrow portion of the competition be worth six points again this year?"

"Yes, Cora, it will."

The girl was about my age, and she had a dark ponytail that went all the way down her back. She was holding a shiny bow and arrow, and the way she handled the thing, it looked like she could take out a sparrow from about thirty yards away.

She caught me looking at her and she *smiled* right at me.

I did what anyone would do when someone holding a bow and arrow smiles at them.

I smiled back.

"Finally, campers," said Mr. Prentice, "as part of Pioneer Day, the whole camp will compete in a favorite game of my ancestors. Tug-of-war!"

Tug-of-war is a game you play when the only
sports equipment you have is a rope.

Mr. Prentice told us we'd be learning more about the tug-of-war later. And we'd also hear all about his ancestors, starting with his great-great-great-great-great-great-grandfather, "the original Sam Prentice," who came to Jamestown from England.

"Now, quickly," said Mr. Prentice, "before it gets dark. Let's divide ye into groups by last names, and meet thy counselors."

Vinny and I spotted a picnic table for kids whose last names began with *R* through *Z*. By the time we reached it, one boy was already there.

"Scot Taylor," said the kid.

I reached out my hand.

"Wait. Hold on. Sorry." The kid pulled a bottle of Purell out of his pocket and smothered his hands with it.

"I'm pretty sure they didn't have that in the 1600s," I said.

"And it's half the reason they died. Disease." Scot aimed the bottle at me. "Want some?"

"Uh, sure," I said, taking the bottle. I didn't want to hurt the kid's feelings. Or get scurvy. Or the plague.

While Vinny, Scot, and I were standing there, a little kid walked up to the picnic table. He couldn't have been more than eight or nine. "Hi, guys," he said in a voice that sounded like a duck on a cartoon. "I'm Perth Wallace. If it's okay with you, I call the bottom bunk."

We all nodded yes.

"Thanks," said Perth. "It's just that the bottom bunk is a little closer to the outhouses. And I'm still working on some, uh, issues."

I couldn't help but wonder why Perth's parents would send him to sleepaway camp, let alone one with outhouses and no electricity.

A tall skinny guy with long hair walked up to our table. He was about seventeen and was wearing the same T-shirt as all the other counselors.

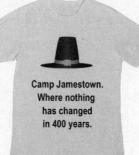

Camp Jamestown.
Where nothing
has changed
in 400 years.

"Hello, men. I'm Theo. We'll be in Cabin Two. Down by the pond. Why don't you guys eat the rest of the meals you brought from home. Then head over to the cabin to unpack. I'm going to grab some supplies, and I'll see you there in a minute."

Mealtime: Nothing to get excited about
when your mom is a *vegan*.

As soon as we finished eating, everyone raced off to Cabin 2. I tried to keep up with them. But the wheels of my cart got *stuck* in the dirt.

"Uhhh, uhhh." I grunted and groaned, trying to get the wheels unstuck.

"Need some help there, *Cartboy?*"

The hair on the back of my neck stood up as I turned to face the person who was talking.

Six feet tall, 180 pounds, most of it muscle.

As Ryan Horner's squinty eyes bore a hole right through me, three other words about Camp Jamestown came to mind.

Must.   Escape.   Now.

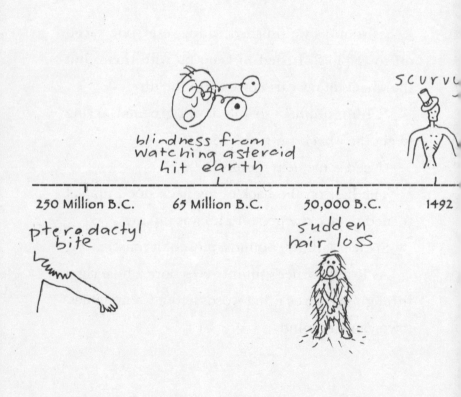

blindness from
watching asteroid
hit earth

scurvy

250 Million B.C.	65 Million B.C.	50,000 B.C.	1492

pterodactyl
bite

sudden
hair loss

o Get Out Of Camp

scarlet fever

yellow fever

hay fever

Bieber fever

1880   1920   1950   2009   Future

intergalactic jet lag

Cabin 2

Dear Alien Who I'm Praying Can Get Me
Out of Here:

I tried to back up. To take tiny steps away from Ryan
Horner. But I didn't get far. My back bumped into a
knotty pine tree right behind me.

"Where do you think you're going, Cartboy?"

"T-t-to the uh . . ."

"I'll tell you where you're going. You're going to
listen to me. And you're going to listen good."

I turned my ears toward Ryan and squinted
my eyes half-closed. As if somehow that would
help.

"The only reason I'm at this dump is because of

you. Because *you* were the one who told on me for cheating on the history test."

I thought about telling Ryan how it wasn't me who told on him. How the only reason I was talking with Mr. Tupkin at the end of the year was to find out my history grade.

But then I remembered the Sweatpants Wedgie.

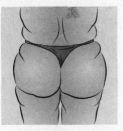

My mouth stayed shut.

Ryan leaned in so close to me, I could feel his breath on my face. "My parents sent me to this camp as punishment. So what I'm going to do is punish you. You will be my personal slave. You will do whatever I tell you to do. The whole time we're here."

"W-won't p-people think it's weird that I'm your slave?"

"As far as you're concerned, Cartboy, I have a

twisted ankle. I'll need to rest the whole time. In that hammock by my cabin."

He pointed to a run-down-looking cabin at the edge of camp, near some dark and creepy woods. Behind the cabin, a hammock was tied between two trees.

The sun was starting to set, and the tree branches cast so many black shadows over the hammock, it looked like a *horror* movie.

"One last thing," said Ryan, pulling my collar up to my chin. "If you tell anyone, I'll give you another wedgie. And this time, your underwear is going to come out your ears."

Ryan loosened his grip on my collar. I took that as a sign to get out of there. Fast.

I ran all the way to Cabin 2 without stopping

once. Even though I was shaking like a wet poodle and my old-lady cart was squeaking behind me the entire way.

Weird.

I sprinted inside the cabin door and sat on the first bunk bed I saw. I must have been shaking pretty hard because Scot leaned over the top bunk and said, "What's the matter, Hal?"

"N-nothing. It's just that, I ran into a big, ugly, hairy, um . . . spider."

"Did you touch it?" he asked, holding out the Purell.

"If it makes you feel any better, Hal, I'm scared of spiders too." Perth was unpacking his bag onto the bottom bunk next to mine.

"Spiders, ants, beetles. Just looking at a bug gives me diarrhea."

He placed a pile of NightTime diapers on the table between our beds. "Feel free to borrow them if you like."

The amount of diapers I'll need every time I see Ryan Horner.

I sat there trying to catch my breath, and for the first time, I had a look around Cabin 2.

The ceiling and floors were made of splintery, jagged logs, and the walls were some sort of combination of dirt and sticks. Mostly, the whole cabin was so old, you could practically see through the cracks to the outside.

Let's just say it was pretty breezy in there.

I spotted Vinny in the corner, sitting on the floor with his map. He looked up at Scot, Perth, and me. "You're all going to need to calm down," he said. "You need your nerves for the treasure hunt."

"Treasure?" yelled Scot.

"What treasure?" asked Perth.

"It was buried by Mr. Prentice's ancestor, Sam Prentice," Vinny said.

"You mean the guy who first came here off the ship?" asked Scot.

"Yes. I found a page of his diary in the camp museum a few years ago. He buried pearls so he could use them to trade with the Indians."

Vinny pointed to a spot on the map, behind the Museum of Colonial Artifacts. "I've searched the whole camp, except this one place. The treasure *has* to be buried there."

"I've got a brand-new shovel," said Scot, pointing to his camp pack. "Count me in. The first thing I'm buying with the treasure money is tickets to One Direction."

One Direction, Backstreet Boys, 'N Sync, or Jonas Brothers? No one knows for sure.

"I'm in too," Perth said to Vinny. "I've got a whole list of stuff I want to buy. Three-speed bike, mood ring, Rainbow Loom, Pop Rocks, Fiddle Faddle, Double Stuf Oreos . . ."

Perth listed about a thousand things, and the whole time he was talking, he was rubbing his stomach. When he finished his list, he let go a huge *fart*. "Ooof. Maybe a little Pepto too," he said.

Meanwhile, I sat there listening. And seeing the profits *diminishing* before my eyes.

I sat down next to Vinny and whispered in his ear. "What about all the money? If we let Scot and Perth hunt with us, we'll have to divide it by four. I don't know about you, but I'm guessing one quarter of a scooter is not that easy to ride."

The last guy who tried to ride
one quarter of a scooter.

"I hear you, Hal," said Vinny. "Dividing the treasure four ways will be less money for us. And Scot and Perth do seem a little, um, high-strung. But this time, I'm not going home without it. We need all the help we can get."

I had to admit, Vinny had a point. We didn't have much time to hunt. There were so many activities and chores.

"So what do you say, guys?" said Vinny. "All in for the treasure hunt?"

Scot, Perth, Vinny, and I made a four-way handshake. "Let's just make sure no one else knows," I said. "It'll be our secret—"

"Sorry I'm late."

We all turned to see Theo walk into the cabin.

"I was helping that Ryan Horner kid. I guess he hurt his foot."

Only one thing was wrong with Ryan's feet: the smell.

Theo put his duffel bag on one of the beds. "Shouldn't you guys be unpacking?"

Everyone emptied their bags, and Cabin 2 suddenly looked like the camping aisle at Denby's, filled with brand-new sleeping bags, LED flashlights, and shiny titanium mess kits and tools and shovels.

With no other choice, I grabbed the bottom of my bag and tried to turn it upside down. Theo must have seen how heavy it was, because he jumped in to help.

"Sorry, Theo," I said, attempting to pick up my dad's leaden ax and Grampa Janson's "World War II Edition" flashlight.

"No worries. Looks like you've got some nice antiques in there."

"If by antiques you meant stuff that's been in my family since the dinosaur age, then yes."

"I've got a family heirloom too." Theo reached in his bag and pulled out an old feathered cap. "This was my grandfather's. It's irreplaceable."

"Are you sure? Because I saw one just like it in the costume section at Bargain Basement."

$4.99

"Ha. You're funny, Hal."

The thing is, I wasn't trying to be funny. I just

didn't see how a dusty old cap could be so valuable. Especially one with a hole in the top. And loose threads everywhere.

While everyone put most of their gear under their beds, Theo explained that we would have to get up around 6 A.M. for breakfast. And that we needed to start practicing for Pioneer Day right away.

Then he told us how it works.

"Up to six points are awarded for each activity. But instead of points, Mr. Prentice uses little Pilgrim hats. A few of the activities, like the bow-and-arrow contest and the tug-of-war, are worth up to six hats. The cabin with the most hats wins."

▲   Might not survive winter.

▲ ▲   Moderate chance of living.

▲ ▲ ▲   Could make it to the first Thanksgiving.

▲ ▲ ▲ ▲   A true pioneer.

Theo quickly unpacked his duffel bag and lay down in his bed. "We better get some sleep," he said.

"Do we really have to get up at six?" I asked.

"No."

"Oh good," I said with a big sigh of relief.

"Mr. Prentice blows the gourd at five forty-five A.M."

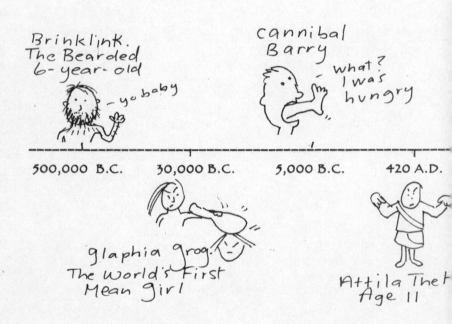

Brinklink.
The Bearded
6- year- old
— yo baby

cannibal
Barry
— what?
I was
hungry

500,000 B.C.   30,000 B.C.   5,000 B.C.   420 A.D.

glaphia grog.
The World's First
Mean girl

Attila The H
Age 11

The Pioneer Life

Dear Possible Owner of a Real Working
Time Machine:

One thing I learned pretty quickly at Camp Jamestown is that 5:45 A.M. means 5:45 A.M.

And not a minute later.

Doo Do Do Looo!

The sound of Mr. Prentice's gourd nearly
knocked me out of my bunk.

Vinny, Scot, Perth, and I stumbled out of bed
and followed Theo to the dining hall. I was pretty
surprised we made it there. Considering our eyes

were half-closed. And Perth had put his shoes on the wrong feet.

We sat at a long wooden table, next to a bunch of girls from Cabin 6, and looked around to see what we were going to eat. I was hoping for something hot and yummy. Like a waffle with whipped cream. Or a cinnamon Dunk-a-Roo.

But breakfast was just like the rest of camp.

About four hundred years old.

I sat there wondering if it was legal to serve kids glue, when suddenly I heard a voice in my ear.

"Cartboy, get me some food."

And then, another voice.

"Shee if you can find shum shaushages shum-where."

I looked up to see not just Ryan, but another kid standing next to him. The kid was even bigger than Ryan, and he was missing about five teeth.

"And shhhhtep on it, Cartboy," he said.

I tapped Vinny on the shoulder and pointed behind me. "Who's that?"

"Ninth-grader. Billy Bendigan. They call him Billy the Bully."

"What happened to his teeth?"

"I heard he lost them in a fight at school. Apparently it involved two fists, a rolled-up gym towel, and an algebra textbook. Let's just say you do not want anything to do with him."

Pre-Algebra. Weighing in at a life-threatening 12.7 pounds.

Ryan shoved his plate in my face. "Get goin', Cartboy."

I walked to the other side of the dining room, filled up Billy's and Ryan's plates, and brought them back to their table.

"Ooh, thank you, Cartboy," said Ryan in a fake, singsongy voice. "I really wish I could have gotten it myself. But, ouch, my ankle hurts sooo much."

With that, Ryan and Billy fell on themselves laughing.

Amount of spit that comes out
when Billy the Bully laughs.

Ryan and Billy stopped laughing when Mr. Prentice appeared at the dining hall door.

He was wearing the same wool coat as the day before, and he had the gourd tucked under his arm. "Good morrow, Jamestown settlers!" he yelled.

"Two minutes till thy first activity! Gather ye in the clearing."

All the kids finished eating and walked over to the far side of the clearing. There was a pile of logs about ten feet high, and Mr. Prentice was standing in front of it.

"Now," he said, grabbing a log off the pile. "Who can tell me the first thing the settlers did when they arrived in Jamestown, Virginia?"

Once again, for reasons I can't begin to understand, he pointed right at me. "Mr. Rifkind. What do you think the settlers did first?"

"Um, went to the bathroom?"

"Try again."

"Took a nap?"

"No."

"Had a snack?"

"Mother of Moccasins! Mr. Rifkind, the answer

is build shelters! The settlers needed a place to live. So they cut down trees to make wood for their cabins. Today, ye shall do the same."

While the counselors handed out axes, Mr. Prentice explained how the settlers made their homes.

"They used a system called wattle and daub," he said. "The wattle was a frame made of thin strips of wood. The daub was the wall, made of soil and clay. A thick wooden frame held the wattle and daub together."

That explains why our cabin is so breezy.

Theo handed out a few axes and started going over the rules of ax safety. He told us we needed to hold the ax at arm's length at all times. And keep the sheath on when we weren't using it. But I was hardly listening.

I was watching Cora pull a piece of wood off the pile. Judging by the size of her biceps, I was pretty sure she could wattle and daub a baseball stadium.

Once again, Cora saw me looking at her. Except this time, she took it as a sign to *walk up to me* and start *talking*.

"I wish the guy who built my cabin had known how to cut wood straight. It's like the Tunnel of Wind at Great Adventure," she said.

"Except you don't have to wait on line for ninety minutes."

Cora stepped even *closer* to me. "I'm guessing this is your first time here. I could show you how to chop wood. Seeing as how you're a rookie and all."

"N-no thanks. I'm good. A good axer. Excellent chopper. First-rate."

"Great. Let's have a race. On your mark, get set, go!"

Cora grabbed some logs and raised her ax. With no other choice, I did the same. And before I knew it, there was a lot of fast and furious chopping.

CHOP CHOP CHOP
CHOP CHOP CHOP
CHOP CHOP CHOP

Sadly, it was all done by Cora.

My ax pretty much got stuck in a log on the first swing. I never did get it out.

The good news was, now I knew what my gym teacher, Mr. Pendle, meant when he said I had "no muscle tone discernible to the human eye."

After a couple of hours, Mr. Prentice came by to check on our progress. He examined Cora's nicely cut logs, piled in a neat stack.

"Four hats for thee!"

Mr. Prentice walked over to me and took a look at my ax stuck in the log. "Jesus, Brother of Crispus" was all he managed to say.

I could tell the number of hats he'd be giving me.

O

After Mr. Prentice left, Theo walked up and put his hand on my shoulder. "Next time, why don't you use your dad's ax, Hal? The one in your camp pack. It's a beauty. Looks like it's been in your family for generations."

Theo started talking about the importance of family heirlooms. A good ten minutes went by, and he was still explaining why his grandfather's feathered cap was "irreplaceable." Luckily, I was saved by the gourd.

It was time for lunch.

This time, I walked into the dining room, sized up the situation, and sat as far away from Ryan and Billy as I could. For one thing, I wasn't going to spend the whole time fetching them food. And the other, lunch was beans and corn, and I knew what that meant.

BEANS AND CORN + BILLY'S TEETH + TALK
= MY FACE COVERED IN FOOD

Vinny and Scot grabbed some lunch and sat down next to me. "Did you hear the news?" asked Vinny in a quiet voice. "Today's afternoon activity is digging for artifacts. We can look for the treasure."

"We're gonna be rich, I can feel it," said Scot. "I'm thinking front-row seats for the One Direction concert—"

FAARRT.

We looked up to see Perth standing by our table, adjusting his pants. "Ooof," he said. "Whatever they served for breakfast clogged up the pipes pretty good."

"Maybe lunch will be better?" I asked Perth, holding up a plate of beans.

Perth's answer was quick and to the point.

FAARRRRRT.

By the time we time finished eating, got our shovels, and waited for Perth to use the bathroom, it was already midafternoon.

We had to hurry to the back of the museum. And dig as fast as we could.

We dug and dug and dug. After three hours, not only did we *not* find the treasure, but we didn't find any colonial artifacts either. And the whole time we had to listen to the *squeals of joy* as the other campers uncovered all kinds of stuff from the 1600s.

Like the girl from Cabin 5, who found an arrowhead. And the boy from Cabin 3, who uncovered a silver knife handle buried near the clearing.

I would say he got four hats for it. But the handle had s. PRENTICE etched on one side. So I'm going with *five*.

🎩 🎩 🎩 🎩 🎩 Going to pioneer heaven.

By the time the gourd sounded for dinner, I was beyond hungry. So I sprinted to the dining hall as fast as I could.

I planned on going to the same table where I'd sat during lunch. The one that was far from Ryan and Billy. But I never made it there.

Seeing as how Ryan *tripped* me as I walked through the door.

"Not so fast, Cartboy."

He "helped" me up, then pulled my face toward his. "There's not enough food at this place. And I need food. You're gonna take one bite of your dinner, then sneak the rest to me."

Like clockwork, Billy appeared at Ryan's side. "And ssssneak me sssome too."

I stared up at Ryan and Billy, drooling over the thought of eating my dinner, and I couldn't help but think of Arnie back at home.

Safely in his room. Playing *RavenCave*. Feasting on doughnuts. Sleeping until noon.

I also couldn't help but think that after just one day at camp, I was already on my way to becoming a real Jamestown settler:

Someone who starves to death.

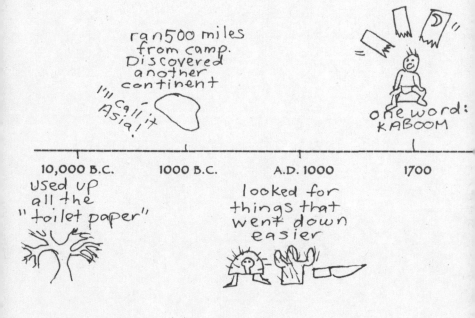

ran 500 miles from camp. Discovered another continent

"I'll call it Asia!"

one word: KABOOM

| 10,000 B.C. | 1000 B.C. | A.D. 1000 | 1700 |

Used up all the "toilet paper"

looked for things that went down easier

:ating Camp Food over Time

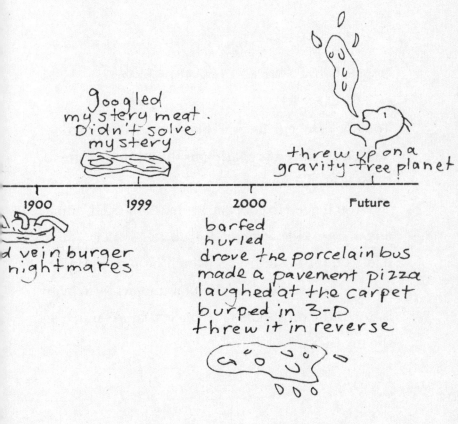

googled
mystery meat.
Didn't solve
mystery

threw up on a
gravity-free planet

1900   1999   2000   Future

d vein burger
nightmares

barfed
hurled
drove the porcelain bus
made a pavement pizza
laughed at the carpet
burped in 3-D
threw it in reverse

Hunting, Digging, and Cake

Dear Possible Driver of a Time-Traveling Vehicle:

Today's first activity was bow-and-arrow practice, and Theo started preparing us the minute we got to breakfast.

"You'll need to concentrate hard," he said. "Bow-and-arrow skills were critical to the settlers. They had to hunt to survive. So you'll be judged on accuracy. And remember, the bow-and-arrow activity is worth the most hats on Pioneer Day. As much as the tug-of-war."

As soon as breakfast was over, Mr. Prentice told us to meet him near the pond, where the bow-and-arrow practice would take place.

All I knew was that this time, if he asked a question, I was not going to answer it. No matter what, I was going to make sure he didn't point to me.

So the minute I got to the pond, I scoped out a good hiding place. Right away I spotted one. It was behind some cattails, not too far from the grassy area where campers were gathered.

It was pretty mosquitoey back there, but I figured, what's a few itchy bites compared to being humiliated in front of fifty kids?

Mr. Prentice blew the gourd and then faced the campers. "As ye know," he said, "the settlers needed

79

meat to supplement their diets. Who amongst thee can name the wild Virginia game which they hunted?"

I tucked even farther into the cattails. Maybe, I thought, Mr. Prentice would point to Vinny or Scot. Or a kid from another cabin.

I stood there, waiting for someone to answer the question. And that's when the mosquito bit me in the face. My hand hit my head with a *slap*.

And Mr. Prentice pointed straight at me. "Mr. Rifkind!"

"What? No. There was a mosquito—"

"Your answer, please. Name the game native to Virginia?"

"Uh. Game?"

"Yes. I'm waiting."

"Baseball?"

"Try again. Think wild game."

"Rugby."

"No! One more try. 'Wild game' is an *animal*."

By this time, most of the kids were laughing. So

I thought hard. Something that lives in bushes and trees and tastes gamey. What could it be?

"I've got it, sir," I said. "Parrots."

"Mary Mother of Smoke Signals!"

Before Mr. Prentice could say anything else, Cora raised her hand. "Raccoon, opossum, black bear, white-tailed deer, and small woodland animals such as squirrels and skunks," she said.

"Correct. Now ye shall practice your shooting."

I was pretty relieved to see Mr. Prentice and a bunch of counselors pull some paper targets out from a storage shed. The targets had silhouettes of animals on them. So we wouldn't have to shoot the real thing. So nothing would get hurt.

Easy for you to say...

Of course, hunting and shooting were not a problem for Ryan Horner.

Somehow, he had managed to "limp" down to the pond. I guess he couldn't resist the opportunity to hurt a living creature. Even if it was just a *picture* of one.

Ryan didn't hit a single target. But he got *three* hats. "Thee has braved an injury and hunted for the good of the settlement, Mr. Horner," I heard Mr. Prentice say.

Our cabin would have done a lot better if it wasn't for me. As it turns out, I am not actually able to aim a bow. Or shoot an arrow. Or concentrate hard.

MY CABIN'S SCORE

Vinny: 3   Scot: 2   Perth: 2   Me: 0

"Don't worry about it, Hal. I have some good news," Vinny said as soon as we sat down for lunch. "The afternoon activity is Free Time. We can do any pioneer activity we like."

Right away, Vinny, Scot, Perth, and I knew what that meant: digging. We ate fast and ran to our cabin for our shovels.

But mine was stuck in the bottom of my pack. "I'll meet you guys behind the museum," I said.

After a good *ten minutes* of tugging and pulling, I hoisted my dad's old shovel out of the moldy green bag and ran toward the back of the museum.

Just as I passed the woodpile at the edge of the clearing, I heard a girl's voice.

"Hal?"

"Oh, hey, Cora," I said. I tried to keep on running.

"Wait. I see you have your shovel—"

"Yep. Shovel. Gotta dig. Bye."

"Hold on. While you're digging for artifacts,

could you keep your eyes peeled for arrowheads? We need them for decorations for the dance."

I stopped in my tracks. "D-d-dance?"

"The theme is the Powhatan Tribes of Virginia. It's on the last night of camp. Are you going?"

"D-dances are not really my thing . . ." I started to say.

It looked like Cora was gonna ask me to go *with her,* so I did what any sensible man would do when a girl is about to ask him out. Hightailed it out of there as fast as I could.

Olympic sprinter Jim Hines ran a hundred meters in 9.95 seconds. I'm pretty sure he heard about the dance too.

When I got to the back of the museum, the guys had already started digging. By the looks of things, they hadn't found anything yet.

So once again, we dug and dug. We dug until Scot's hands were covered in dirt. Perth got a stomachache. And I got a blister the size of a quarter.

"Maybe someone already found the pearls and took them," said Scot, throwing down his shovel.

"Maybe that Sam what's-his-name never buried it," said Perth.

"Maybe you should tell us exactly what makes you think there is a treasure, Vinny," I said.

Vinny put his shovel on the ground and pulled a small paper out of his pocket. "This is what I found in the Museum of Colonial Artifacts a few years ago. It's the page from Sam Prentice's dairy. Here."

September 1607
The trove of pearls are buried within the walls of the Prentice compound. I hid them lest we needeth them to trade with the

Powhatans for food. As the crops are thin
and the winter grows bitter cold.

"It was even signed," said Vinny, pointing to the bottom of the paper.

Sam Prentice's handwriting reminds me of when Bea
and Perrie get ahold of my mom's lipstick.

"Well, maybe it's not buried behind the museum," said Scot.

Vinny put the piece of paper back in his pocket. "I looked everywhere else."

"Well, it's not here."

"Let's not panic," I said. "Where else could it be? Maybe we can find another clue."

"The thing is," said Vinny, "I looked through every shelf of the museum. The diary this page came from is gone."

I'm guessing Sam Prentice's diary did not look like this.

All the way to dinner, and all during dinner, we argued about what to do next.

"I say we call off the hunt," said Perth.

"I say we keep looking," said Scot.

"I say we keep looking only if we find another clue."

We all agreed to hunt for another clue. But we kept arguing over where to find one. We argued so much, we forgot to listen to Mr. Prentice's dinner-time lecture on wilderness survival.

I vaguely heard him say something about using a stick and the sun for a compass. And mention which plants were edible.

It wasn't until Mr. Prentice's lecture was over that my ears finally perked up. "And now, it's time for mail delivery!" he said.

My heart skipped a beat when a counselor handed me a letter.

It was from Arnie. It had to be. He said he was going to send me the sports section so I could see how the Phillies were doing. And that he'd try to sneak in a couple of baseball cards and gum.

I ripped open the envelope and pulled the letter out as fast as I could.

Not only was it not from Arnie. It was from my *dad*. He said my *whole family* would be coming for Pioneer Day. And that he knows I can "win the competition."

The first thing that came to my mind was that there were two people my dad had never met:

1. Cora.   2. Me.

I wanted to lie down on the splintery floor of the dining room and *sob*. I actually was going to do it. But just then, my eye caught something that could make me forget about my dad's letter. The missing treasure. And my chances of winning Pioneer Day.

Solves any problem you are having in the first bite.

Theo must have seen me staring at the table of chocolate cake with my mouth hanging open, because he came over and sat down next to me.

"Every once in a while," he said, "Mr. Prentice serves dessert as a special treat. It makes the campers happy. That, and if you go home too skinny, he gets in trouble."

I took a piece of cake from the dessert table and carried it to the front steps of the dining hall.

Outside, the cool air filled my lungs.

As I lifted a bite of the creamy chocolate to my mouth, I felt myself relax for the first time since I got here. I felt like somehow, some way, everything might be okay. I might actually survive.

The feeling lasted about one minute. Right up until Ryan grabbed the cake out of my hands.

Things Kids Have Snuck Int

gummy
dinosaurs

their
pet rock

153 Million B.C.   31,563 B.C.   10,562 B.C.   997 B.C.

head-to-toe
lice

their too

party
in my
cabin!

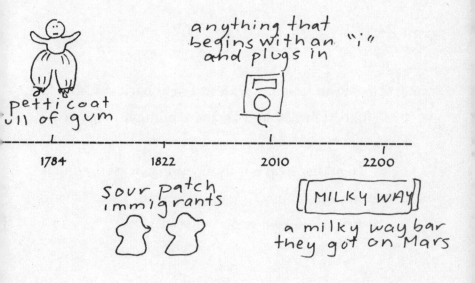

anything that
begins with an "i"
and plugs in

petticoat
ull of gum

1784   1822   2010   2200

sour patch
immigrants

[MILKY WAY]
a milky way bar
they got on Mars

A CLUE

Dear ?:

After Ryan stole my dessert, I went back to Cabin 2. I climbed in bed and lay there all night long. Wide awake.

I couldn't help but think, well, at least my dad is getting his money's worth. After all, I was having the full Jamestown experience:

sugar-deprived ✔

arms feel like lead ✔

covered in blisters ✔

losing fight with enemy ✔

feel like made mistake ✔

want to go home ✔

By the time the gourd blew at five forty-five, I was sure of one thing: I was not going to the day's first activity. No matter what it was.

Doo Do Do Looo!

"Up and at 'em," said Theo. "C'mon, Hal."

"Unhh."

"We're going straight to the museum after breakfast!"

"Unhhnh. Just want sleep."

From the sound of things, Scot and Perth weren't budging either. "Us too," they mumbled.

"We'll be beading leather in the museum! It's good fun!"

Even Vinny buried his face under his pillow. "What's the point, Theo?" he said. "It's not like our cabin has the slightest chance of winning Pioneer Day."

Theo sat on the end of my bed and took a deep breath. "Maybe your scores haven't been too high, guys. But there's lots more stuff to do. Carving canoes. Yarn spinning. Churning butter. And don't forget, we've got to practice for the tug-of-war!"

The amount of combined arm strength in Cabin 2.

I dragged my feet out of bed, trudged over to the dining hall, and forced the gluey glop down my throat.

After breakfast, we slogged over to the Museum of Colonial Artifacts. As soon as we got inside, I plunked down in an antique wooden chair in the back corner. Maybe, I thought, I could catch some sleep while everyone else did their beadwork.

Makes a good pillow when you are desperate enough.

After about a minute, Mr. Prentice appeared at the museum door. He held up a small square of something dark and leathery.

"As many of thee know," he said, "the Powhatan Indians wore clothing made from animal skins. They used needles made of bone to sew through the tough hides. And decorated the skins with beads."

He stepped a little farther into the museum. "The Powhatan's bead designs included clouds, animals, trees—all the things they loved. My question for thee is, what design was the favorite of the Powhatans?"

Mr. Prentice took a few steps in my direction. Here we go again, I thought. He is going to point to me.

And sure enough, he walked right past the girls in Cabins 5, 6, and 7, and stopped dangerously close to my napping chair.

"Mr. Rifkind. This time I shall give thee a hint. The favorite design of the Powhatans is something you see on a dollar bill."

I breathed a huge sigh of relief. Finally, I knew the answer. Finally, I would not be embarrassed in front of the entire camp.

"George Washington," I said.

When Mr. Prentice heard my answer, he stayed pretty quiet. He kind of hung his head down and muttered to himself. I couldn't be sure, but I think I heard something along the lines of, "Holy Hanger of Deerskins, what is wrong with that kid?"

Theo handed out the animal hides, beads, thread, and bone needles to Scot, Vinny, Perth, and me. He explained that the favorite design of the Powhatans was the bald eagle. But that we could do whatever we wanted. "Leather beading is worth four hats on Pioneer Day. You'll be judged on design concept and overall beading skill," he said.

While Theo gave out the supplies, I took a look around the museum. And while I was looking, I realized something: I'd been so busy digging behind the museum, I'd never been inside it.

Every wall was covered with shelves full of old stuff. Indian headdresses. Jewelry. Authentic documents. And a bunch of musty colonial clothes.

One wall had a whole section for past winners of Pioneer Day. My dad's name was right there. Underneath his wood carving of the original Sam Prentice.

If you ask me, it looked a lot like my uncle Lou.

I noticed the other campers had started sewing bead designs onto their leather. Clouds, trees. All the stuff Mr. Prentice told us the Powhatans liked.

I was just sitting there, so I figured I'd sew the letter *P* onto the leather. Just to kill some time. But the funny thing was, once I started sewing those beads, I realized I was almost, sort-of good at it.

My design was just about done when Mr. Prentice walked by.

"Ah, yes. The letter *P* for the mighty Powhatans. Magnificent idea, Mr. Rifkind."

The P was actually for the Philadelphia Phillies, but that was a detail Mr. Prentice didn't need to know.

When he got to Cora's table, Mr. Prentice took a long look at her design. "Let's see," he said. "It's a uh, um, uh . . ."

"It's a butterfly, Mr. Prentice. Can't you tell?" Cora lifted up the animal hide. "One of my ancestors was a Powhatan. Her name was Aponi. It means 'dancing butterfly.'"

I thought I heard a slight quiver in her voice.

Could it be that Cora was not good at something? And I was? Could that actually be possible?

While Mr. Prentice and Cora talked, I took a break from my beading. For one thing, I was almost done with my Phillies logo. And for the other, trying to get that bone needle through the leather was *killing* my fingers.

I walked to the shelves on the back wall of the museum. They were full of books, and there was a whole section called "The First Settlers."

I picked up a few of the books and skimmed some of the pages. A bunch of time must have passed while I was looking at those books. Before I knew it, the gourd blew for lunch.

Doo Do Do Looo!

"You coming, Hal?" asked Vinny on the way out.

"I'll be there in a minute."

Everyone put their beadwork on a shelf and left the museum. All of a sudden, it was completely quiet.

It was just me in there. With all that old colonial stuff.

I could have sworn Uncle Lou was
staring at me wherever I went.

I walked toward the shelf to put my beading proj-
ect away. But when I got near it, my foot kicked a
chair. At least I thought it was a chair. So I was pretty
surprised when I looked down and saw it was a book.

It must have fallen off the shelves.

I picked it up. The pages were super yellow and
faded-looking. The handwriting was the same as
the page Vinny showed us. And there was a signa-
ture inside the back cover.

My heart started racing like crazy. Could this
be the book Vinny was looking for? Could this be
the rest of Sam Prentice's journal?

I quickly glanced around the museum to make sure no one was around. Then I sat in my chair and flipped through the pages.

It turns out, Sam Prentice was a super-hard worker. He tried everything he could to harvest the settlement's pathetic crops. He hunted every day. And built a wattle-and-daub cabin for his family.

He also tried to make peaceful trades with the Powhatans. And—this part really caught my eye—he *buried* stuff to trade with them later.

Sam Prentice's last diary entry said how so many people in Jamestown were starving. Near the end of the diary, his handwriting got even worse. By the looks of things, he never made it. And neither did his family.

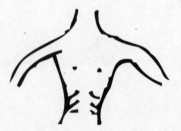

The Jamestown Diet.
Works every time.

My hands started to shake when I saw what was at the bottom of the last page.

Pearls 500 feet west
of the Big Ben

I hid the book in my pocket, then ran out the museum door. My feet couldn't carry me to the dining hall fast enough.

I think I made it there in 9.95 seconds.

I didn't see Ryan and Billy anywhere. But just to be safe, I ducked down so those two food-grubbers wouldn't notice me.

"Guys," I whispered when I got to my table.

"Look at this." I pulled the diary out of my pocket and opened it to the last page.

Vinny was the first to say something. "Holy. Jeez."

"Five hundred feet west of the B. E.?" said Perth.

"The handwriting isn't clear," I said. "He must have been weak from hunger. Or maybe the ink faded. Either way, we have to figure out what the B. E. is."

The guys had all kinds of intelligent suggestions:

"Wait a second," said Vinny. "What about the big elm? There's only one elm tree at camp. It's near the edge of the clearing. I even have it on my map."

We ran from the dining room to the big elm. Then, together we started walking west. Putting one foot in front of the other, and counting out loud with every step.

"One—two—three." And then, after a few minutes, "one hundred—two hundred—three hundred . . ." Until finally we were almost there.

"Four ninety-seven . . . four ninety-eight . . . four ninety-nine—"

We all stopped dead in our tracks.

Exactly five hundred feet from the big elm was Ryan Horner's hammock.

With who else lying in it, but Ryan Horner.

"You better tell me why you're here, Cartboy," he said.

Prizes Awarded For Cam

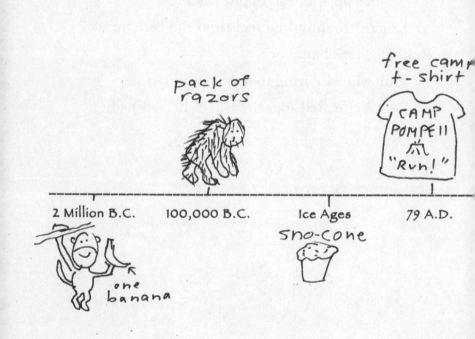

free camp
t-shirt

pack of
razors

CAMP
POMPEII
"Run!"

2 Million B.C.   100,000 B.C.   Ice Ages   79 A.D.

sno-cone

one
banana

Competitions Over Time

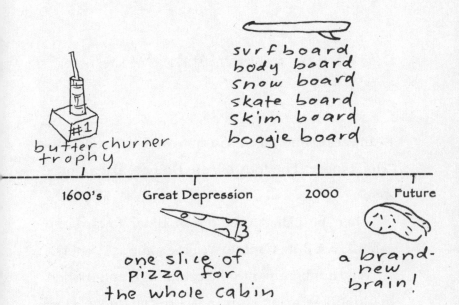

butter churner
trophy

surfboard
body board
snow board
skate board
skim board
boogie board

1600's   Great Depression   2000   Future

one slice of
pizza for
the whole cabin

a brand-
new
brain!

Night Hunting

Dear Future Person Who Might Have My Life
in Their Hands:

Ryan sat up and faced Vinny, Scot, Perth, and me.
"Don't move. The four of you. Do not take a single
step."

Then he called over his shoulder toward the
cabin. "Hey, Billy. C'mere. We have some . . . visitors."

Billy lumbered onto the cabin steps and flashed
his toothless grin. "You mean treshpashers. How
'bout I teach 'em a lessssson?"

Billy's meaty foot stepped toward us, so we turned
around and ran.

All the way to our cabin. Without stopping.

The second we got inside, we collapsed onto our bunks. Scot had barely reached his bed before he grabbed the bottle of Purell.

He started slathering the Purell not just on his hands, but his *arms* too. As if it would wash away Ryan and Billy and the whole situation. "I'll never get those tickets to One Direction now," he said.

Perth dropped onto the bed next to mine. "There goes my three-speed bike. And the mood ring. And the Rainbow Loom. Not to mention the Double Stuf Oreos . . ."

"Front row. I would have been twenty feet from Harry. And Liam. And Zayn . . ."

Perth grabbed his stomach. "Uhhgh. This is not helping the digestive system."

FAARRT.

The whole time Scot and Perth were talking, Vinny stayed quiet. I could tell he was thinking about what to do next. Finally he looked up at me.

"I hate to give up the hunt, Hal. But let's face it. Ryan is in that hammock *all day*."

"True." I took a deep breath. "But . . . he's not there at night."

"What are you saying, Hal? That we dig in the middle of the night?"

"We could."

Perth sat straight up. "That's crazy. First of all, we'd have to sneak past Theo. Just the thought of it gives me indigestion."

FAAAAARRRT.

Our cabin was starting to smell
worse than Ryan's feet.

"Besides," said Vinny, "we'd have to dig in the dark."

I sat back on my bed and let out a big sigh. Vinny was right. Digging in the dark was a really dumb idea.

I was about to give up on the treasure too. But right at that second, I looked over at my cart. It was sitting in the corner of the cabin. Folded up. As if it were waiting for me to take it to school next year. To torture me even more.

I stood up, faced the guys, and cleared my throat. "Vinny. The first day of camp, what did you say about going home with the treasure?"

"That I wasn't leaving without it."

"And Scot, you just said how badly you want those concert tickets."

"True."

"And Perth. Just think: Pepto-Bismol. By the case. By the truckload, even."

"Unhhhnnh," said Perth from the bottom bunk next to mine.

Vinny ran his fingers along his rolled-up map. "We *do* know the treasure's exact location now. I mean, it's almost like we have to see if it's there."

"Okay, then it's settled," I said. "We leave at midnight. When Ryan, Billy, Theo, and the whole camp will be sound asleep."

Just then, the wind knocked a tree branch into the side of our cabin. "I don't know about tonight, Hal," said Vinny. "Sounds like the wind is really picking up out there. I think there's a storm coming."

"Well, then, I guess we better dig fast."

One thing we figured out pretty quickly is that even if it's midnight, sneaking past a camp counselor is not easy. Especially one who tosses and turns. And *talks nonstop* in his sleep.

Theo: Has anyone seen the meat ther-
        mometer?
Theo: Hey, Susie, you look nice.
Theo: Mm . . . candy canes . . . Thanks,
        Santa.

After about five false starts, we finally crept past Theo and out the door.

"Remember, everyone: complete silence," I whispered when we got outside the cabin.

FART.

"C'mon, Perth. I know you can do it."

WHOOOOSH.

"Okay, but what was that?"
"Nothing. Just the wind."

"I think the storm is gonna be bad . . ."

"Let's just get to the hammock."

The truth is, I was having a pretty hard time keeping quiet myself. Seeing as how I kept *tripping*. Thanks to my dad's flashlight.

Not only did it weigh about twenty pounds. But it also kept blinking on and off. Knowing my dad, he must have thought fresh batteries were a "needless extravagance."

GRAND TOTAL: $1.49

Finally we reached the hammock and started to dig. Perth managed to quiet down. But I had to admit, it was spooky out there. Majorly spooky.

The wind was *howling* and rain had started to fall.

WHOOOOSH!

A gust of wind whipped a branch across my face.

BANG!

Ryan's hammock flew up and knocked some-thing over.

BOOM. CREAK. GRRRR!

"What was that?" Scot's voice was trembling in the dark. "It s-sounded like a human. Or a wounded animal. Or a wounded human . . ."

"Or a bear," whispered Vinny.

Perth shone his flashlight on Vinny. "D-did you say b-bear?"

"I'm just saying, it's possible," whispered Vinny. "I mean, based on the story of 'The Jamestown Boy Who Disappeared.'"

"What b-boy?" asked Perth.

"Legend has it that a boy disappeared near Camp Jamestown back in the 1700s. He was last seen near the edge of the woods, close to the pond."

Vinny smacked his shovel into the ground and lifted a pile of dirt. "They sent out a search party, but all they found was a patch of brown fur near the woods. Since the Powhatans believed bears had special powers, it was thought the bear took the boy in retaliation for when the settlers stole the Powhatans' food."

"Vinny, that's impossible," I started to say. But just then, my flashlight went out. And wouldn't go back on.

It was so dark, I could hardly see my hand in front of my face. The pitch black made every noise seem ten times louder.

"Let's just keep digging," I said. "C'mon, guys. We are so close. We're ninety percent there."

We dug and dug. But the storm only got worse. The rain beat against our faces, and the wind whipped dirt everywhere.

And then came a noise so deep and low, it went straight to our bones.

GRHHHHHHHRRRRRGRRR...

We looked toward the woods. There, right next to a giant pine tree, was a *huge* shadow. It had a head and arms that looked like they were reaching out to *grab* us.

It was impossible to tell what it was.

And Scot and Perth didn't stay around long enough to find out. They each let out a short scream:

"Ahh!"

"Ahh!"

Then they were gone. Headed back to Cabin 2 as fast as their legs could carry them.

"Should we go after them?" I whispered to Vinny.

"It's no use," he whispered back.

"I guess it's down to us," I said.

My flashlight flicked back on and shone in Vinny's face. He looked wet. Dirty. And completely exhausted.

I could tell it was time to call off the dig for the night. And that if we had one more setback, Vinny would be out too.

Things Kids Have Heard At Night

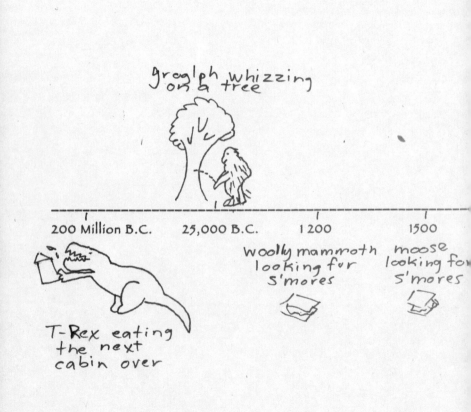

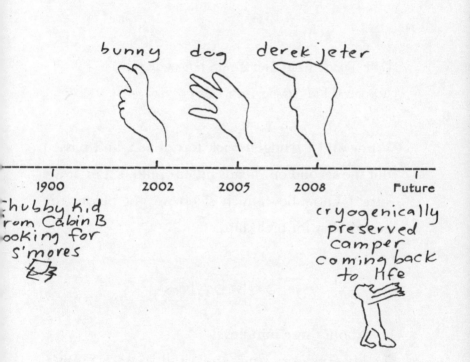

bunny   dog   derek jeter

1900   2002   2005   2008   Future

Chubby kid
from Cabin B
looking for
s'mores

cryogenically
preserved
camper
coming back
to life

Pie

Dear Buddy from Space with Potential
Advanced Kid-Saving Technology:

Vinny and I trudged back to Cabin 2 and passed out the second our heads hit our pillows. I'm pretty sure I know how much sleep we got before the gourd blew for breakfast.

Doo Do Do LOoooo!

About three minutes.

My eyes were stuck shut, and so were Vinny's. But somehow we put our feet on the floor and walked out the door. Somehow, we also managed to follow Theo across the clearing and to the dining hall.

"For some reason," Theo said on the way, "I couldn't wake up Scot and Perth. They must be exhausted from all the practice for Pioneer Day."

"That must be it," I said, trying to pull my eyelids open.

We sat as far from Ryan and Billy as we could. But even though there were twenty kids between us, Vinny and I could still see the two of them talking.

"They must be wondering where all those holes under the hammock came from," Vinny whispered into my ear.

"Let's not wait to find out."

We hightailed it out of the dining room and into the clearing. Partly to avoid any questions from Ryan and Billy.

And partly because we had a lot to do. Pioneer Day was just a few days away. We needed to get in as much practice as we could.

Vinny and I made a list of every activity we really needed to improve on.

**CUTTING WOOD
CARVING CANOES
BEADING LEATHER
BOW & ARROW HUNTING
CHURNING BUTTER
DIGGING FOR ARTIFACTS**

Sadly, the list looked exactly like
Mr. Prentice's scroll.

Since morning was free time, we decided to start with canoe building. A bunch of girls had already set up behind a big log by the pond, so we figured we'd join them.

"We can work on our log carving technique and hide from Ryan and Billy at the same time," I said to Vinny.

As soon as we got to the pond, I grabbed a chisel and tried to gouge out some of the log.

After about ten minutes, the only thing I managed
to gouge out was a piece of my thumb.

"You want some advice?"

I looked up to see Cora standing above me, next to a nicely chiseled section of the log.

"First, you use an ax to scrape the bark off the log. Then you use a chisel to carve a groove in the top."

Cora placed her chisel against the log. "Gently and smoothly. Right down the center. Leave about a foot on either side."

I copied exactly what she did. Over and over again. And by the end of the morning, we had carved out a big hunk of the canoe. It actually started to look like something an Indian would have made in the 1600s.

Not available in the camping aisle at Denby's.

"How is it possible that you could be so good at carving canoes?" I asked Cora. "And chopping wood. And shooting a bow and arrow. And spinning yarn, and—"

"I guess it's in my blood. My ancestor on my mother's side was a Powhatan. Her Indian name was—"

"Dancing butterfly."

"Yes!" Cora stared down at her chisel for a minute—then she looked me in the eyes. "You know, Hal, you're smarter than you think."

"By the way," she said, taking a step closer to me, "have you thought about whether you're going to the dance?"

"Oh, the dance. Well, I, um, uh . . ."

All I knew was the last time I went to a dance was in sixth grade with Cindy Shano. I couldn't think of a *single thing* to say to her the whole way there. And then I spilled a whole glass of punch on my tuxedo T-shirt when she tried to hold my hand.

"Well, Cora, I, um, uh—"

doo doo loot!

As the famous saying goes, I was saved by the gourd.

"Gotta run!" I said.

I put my chisel back on the log, and then sprinted to my table in the dining hall. Compared to all that dance talk, corn and beans actually sounded good.

I had barely finished my plate, when Mr. Prentice appeared at the kitchen door. "Hear ye, hear ye. In celebration of all your hard work in preparing for Pioneer Day, we shall have a very special treat for dessert today."

He wheeled a table out from the kitchen, and my mouth popped open about a mile when I saw what was on it.

The best dessert in the history of the universe: banana cream pie.

Whoever invented banana cream pie knew how to get the proportions right.

My legs, all by themselves, walked to the dessert table. My hands, all on their own, picked up a piece of pie. And my fork dipped itself into the soft whipped cream topping.

The whipped cream would have made it into my mouth. Except for one thing.

"You weren't actually thinking of eating that, were you, Cartboy?"

It took every ounce of energy I had to get the pie moving in Ryan's direction. But when Ryan tried to take the plate, I couldn't release it.

"Give it, Cartboy."

"I c-can't . . ."

"I said give it . . ."

He pulled, but my hand pulled back.

By the time Mr. Prentice walked up to us, we were having a full-on banana cream pie tug-a-thon.

"Mother of Rusty Muskets. What's going on here?"

"Well, Mr. Prentice, Ryan tried to take my—"

Before I could finish, Ryan whispered two little words in my ear.

"Sweatpants. Wedgie."

"—I mean, I was just . . . giving my dessert to Ryan. Banana cream pie is his favorite."

And then my hand released it.

Mr. Prentice looked at Ryan and me. "I'm quite pleased to see ye conducting yeselves with such a generous pioneer spirit. As the great seventeenth-century philosopher, Ernest Dimnet, once said, 'Friends in needeth are friends indeedeth.'"

If you ask me, that Dimwit guy
was pretty clueless.

I ran from the dining hall to the big log pile in the middle of camp and grabbed the first ax I saw. I aimed it at a piece of wood and swung hard.

Yes, I was mad. Yes, I wanted to hit something. And yes, the ax got stuck in the log and I couldn't get it out.

I stood there yanking and pulling. And that's when I noticed Cora had followed me.

"Why didn't you stand up to that guy? Why did you let him trample all over you?"

"It's hard to explain—"

"You want me to get him for you? I'll take that jerk down with one karate chop to the jugular. I'll crack his noggin open so wide, he won't know what hit him. I'll—"

"Maybe just let it go, Cora."

"But—"

"Please."

"Okay. You're right, Hal. Besides, we've got bigger things to talk about. I mean . . . I'm just gonna say it: Will you come with me to the dance?"

"Uh . . ."

"It will be fun. We're decorating the dining hall with tons of Indian artifacts."

"I, um, uh . . ." I stood there wiggling and squirming and trying to think of an answer. "Uh, um . . ."

I was still stalling when I happened to look in the direction of Ryan's hammock. As soon as I saw it, I did a double take.

Even though lunch was over, the hammock was empty. Ryan was nowhere to be found.

I looked all around camp to see where he could be. And then I spotted him. He was on the back steps of the dining hall. Eating a *whole* banana cream pie. And getting a *foot rub* from Billy the Bully.

+ =

Only one type of person can touch Ryan's feet:
one who has ZERO sense of smell.

I looked back at Ryan's empty hammock: This
was our chance. Vinny and I had to go dig.

"What do you say, Hal? Will you go with me?"
Cora asked again.

"Yes. Yes, I'll go." I was so busy looking at Ryan's
hammock, I wasn't sure what I was saying. Did I just
tell Cora I would go with her to the dance?

Whatever I had said, there was no time to think
about it.

"I have to run," I said. "I have to find Vinny."

I sprinted inside the museum, where Vinny was
spinning some yarn.

Gramma Janson has a yarn spindle in her living room. We usually hang our coats on it.

"Vinny. Ryan's hammock is empty. We can dig. Hurry. Let's go."

Vinny looked in the direction of Ryan's hammock and then back at me. "Um, there's no way."

"Look. Ryan is behind the dining hall with Billy. By the looks of things, they'll be busy for at least another half hour."

"No, thanks."

"Vinny, this might be our last chance."

"I know. But if Billy and Ryan catch us, we're dead. Plus, I've been thinking. Maybe the B. E. is not the big elm."

"There's one way to find out." I gave Vinny my most begging-y look.

"Please?" I said.

"Five minutes. I'll go for five minutes and that's it."

We hurried to Cabin 2 and grabbed our shovels. Then we slowly, carefully crept behind all the boys' cabins, looking over our shoulders every *two seconds*.

"Are they coming?"

"No."

"Are you sure?"

"Yes."

"What's Ryan doing?"

"Still eating pie."

As soon as we reached the hammock, we started digging frantically. As if every second counted. Which it did.

After a few minutes, I leaned toward Vinny. "I know this is hard. And scary. But let's look on the bright side: Since Scot and Perth are out, we're back to splitting the treasure fifty–fifty."

"Sixty–forty."

"Right. Luckily those pearls will be worth a lot."

"Pearls?" A deep, low voice came from behind a pine tree near the hammock.

And then Ryan and Billy stepped out.

"What pearls?" said Ryan.

"D-did I say pearls?" I said. "Ha! I was just telling Vinny about my grandmother's pearls. She sold them at a garage sale. Made four bucks!"

Ryan stepped right up to my face. "So that's what all these holes are for. You guys are digging for a buried treasure."

Vinny and I tried to take off. To get out of there before there were any more questions. But Ryan and Billy blocked us like a couple of linebackers for the 49ers.

"Oh, don't stop digging, you two," said Ryan. "Please, carry on. And when you do find those pearls, there are two special people you're going to give them to: us."

"W-what if we don't find them before Pioneer Day?" I asked.

"You'll just have to find a way. Won't you?"

The Best Pioneer

Dear Reader Who I Hope Is Still with Me:

Pioneer Day started out just like every day at Camp Jamestown. I woke up at 5:45 A.M. to a sound that was bone-shattering. Head-splitting. And dangerously close to my ear.

You can hear my dad's car backfire
from up to seven miles away.

My whole family piled out of the car and charged into my cabin like they hadn't seen me in fourteen years. They were shouting and screaming so much, you could barely make out a word they said.

I hadn't even gotten out of *bed* yet.

"How did you get here so early?" I asked my dad.

"We stayed at a nearby motel."

"*You* sprang for a motel?"

"Well, okay, we slept in the car. But it was in a motel parking lot."

I hugged the twins, gave Grampa Janson a low five, and introduced everyone to my bunkmates and Theo.

"You are all invited to breakfast!" Theo said.

We walked to the dining hall and went inside. It was busting at the seams with campers, moms, dads, cousins—you name it.

Seeing as how most of the families had traveled far, and seemed hungry, I thought breakfast would be something special.

But nope. It was the same as always.

One can always dream. . . .

The parents all looked pretty horrified when they tasted the breakfast gruel. But there was one person it didn't bother: my dad. He took a *double* helping and started wolfing it down.

"Incredible!" he said. "It's like we've gone back 'n tme. 'Nd we're livng jst lke th frst sttlrs."

I figured he had trouble getting the vowels out on account of the fact his tongue was *stuck* to the roof of his mouth.

He didn't even stop chewing when he looked up and saw someone he knew. "Ryn Hrnr!"

"Oh. Um. Hey, Mr. Rifkind."

My dad pointed to the seat right *next to mine.* "Wld you lk t join us?"

"Yes, I would." Ryan plunked his blimpy frame down an *inch* away from me. And then he whispered in my ear. "You better find those pearls for me, Cartboy. Today."

"But . . . we've dug up every inch of ground by your hammock. They're not there."

"Then look somewhere else. I don't care where. Just find them—"

Doo Doo Loot!

Ryan quit talking, and everyone turned to see Mr. Prentice standing at the door.

"Welcome, boys, girls, counselors, parents, and history lovers!" he said. "Today, thy campers shall demonstrate everything they have learned over the past two weeks!"

We all followed Mr. Prentice to the middle of the clearing. Once everyone had gathered around him, he pulled out a special Pioneer Day scroll.

"Now," he said. "Each activity shall be awarded up to six points, or pioneer hats. And each shall be judged based on very specific criteria.

Cutting wood	Straightness
Carving canoes	Smoothness
Beading leather	Design and technique
Bow & arrow hunting	Accuracy
Churning butter	Speed
Digging for artifacts	Historic value

"Ye can choose any order ye like to do your activities!" said Mr. Prentice. "I shall walk around and award the scores throughout the day. Begin!"

The campers and their parents scattered like cockroaches in the sun. But I just stood there, frozen, not sure what to do first.

"Why don't you start with bow-and-arrow hunting, Hal?" said my dad. "I'm sure you're good at it."

"Uh . . ."

"That was my specialty when I was here!"

My mom, dad, Grampa Janson, and the twins all followed me to the bow-and-arrow area by the pond. I picked up a bow and thought maybe I'd get lucky. Maybe some of those Rifkind hunting genes would kick in. Right when I needed them most.

I grabbed an arrow, aimed, and started shooting at the target in front of me. It was a silhouette of a squirrel.

My first twelve arrows missed the squirrel completely. Then by some miracle, I got a bull's-eye.

Too bad it was on another camper's target.

It wasn't until one of my arrows nearly took out Grampa Janson's hearing aid that my dad said, "Let's move on."

He looked around at all the colonial activities. "Ooh, how about butter churning, son? I was the fastest at that!"

We all headed to the butter-churning station. When we got there, it turns out Ryan Horner was just finishing up. It also turns out he left a little present for me on the butter churner handle: about a pound of *greasy* butter.

"Try this," said my dad. "It's a churning technique I invented when I was here."

He put both hands in front of him, and pretended they were wrapped around a butter churner handle. "You grab the handle with your thumbs ten inches apart, squeeze hard, and go up and down every three seconds. I even had a name for it: the 'Rifkind Rip.'"

I tried the Rifkind Rip for a good ten minutes. I figured it would help me get at least a couple of hats on my score. But thanks to Ryan's little "gift," all it did was make hands slip off the handle *twice as fast.*

Amount of butter I churned in half an hour.

"Okay, shake it off," said my dad.

He spotted the pile of wood in the clearing. "Let's see you do some wattle and daub, Hal! I bet you're great at that."

A bunch of girls from Cora's cabin had gathered with their families at one end of the woodpile. So my family and I walked to the other end. I grabbed a log off the pile, picked up an ax, and gave it my hardest *chop*.

"I've got it." Cora came over, pulled my ax out of the log, and handed it to me.

"Thanks." I tried to give Cora the "you can go now" look, but she wasn't paying attention. She walked straight up to my mom and dad.

"I'm Cora," she said. "Hal and I are going to the dance together!"

"Oh! Oh my, that's wonderful. Just terrific. Stupendous." My mom practically fell on herself trying to get the compliments out fast enough. She reached out and hugged me like I was three years old. "My big boy!"

My dad, on the other hand, was not shouting any compliments. Or hugging me at all.

He was examining the morning score sheet, which Mr. Prentice had posted on a tree near the woodpile.

"Hmph," was all he said.

My mom and Cora said good-bye and "nice to meet you" for about a hundred years—then my family and I went to lunch.

All through the beans and corn, my dad was pretty quiet. His face looked the same as it does when I get a D on one of Mr. Tupkin's history tests.

I racked my brain to think of some way to improve the situation.

"Let's head to the museum, Dad. I'll show you my leather beading!"

P

The minute we got to the museum, I took my design off the shelf.

"I made the letter *P*."

For the first time since Pioneer Day started, my dad actually smiled.

"Check it out," I said. I unfolded the fabric to show him the rest of the design. Underneath the letter *P*, I had beaded a picture of a hot dog and some Cracker Jacks.

Understandably, some people like baseball just for the food.

My dad's smile disappeared.

"Go Phillies?" I tried.

"Hal. This beadwork has nothing to do with Jamestown settlers. Or Powhatan Indians. Or colonial history of any kind."

"I know, but . . . the Phillies are 15 and 4 . . ."

"And your score on every other activity is zero."

"Yes, well, the thing is—"

"What exactly have you been doing for the past two weeks? Have you not taken history camp seriously for a single minute?"

I could tell my dad was going to launch into one of his speeches about why history is so important. And how history explains who we are and why. Or something like that. So I put my beading on the shelf and headed toward the door.

"Sorry, Dad," I said. "I have to get ready for the tug-of-war."

A History Of Things Invente

thong
underwear

—chomp

sailing

28 Million B.C.   10,000 B.C.   1,000 B.C.   1600

ziplining

whittling
contest =

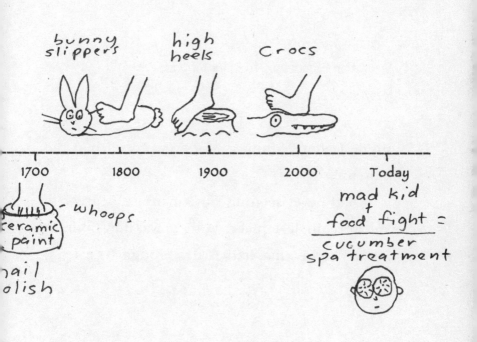

bunny
slippers

high
heels

Crocs

1700   1800   1900   2000   Today

ceramic
paint - whoops

nail
olish

mad kid
    +
food fight =
―――――――――
cucumber
spa treatment

Tug-of-War

Dear Commander of the Hal Rifkind
Rescue Mission:

Inside Cabin 2, things were even worse than the museum.

I had never seen my bunkmates so depressed. We were in last place. And it was my fault. It was *my* score that had really brought the team down.

"Let's just get the tug-of-war over with," I said.

"What if they put us against Ryan Horner? What if I have diarrhea? What if my gas acts up?" Perth was lying on his bed, rubbing his stomach. "I'm scared," he said.

"Tell me about it," said Scot. "Everyone here is going to put their grubby paws on that rope. It'll be *covered* in germs. Rotavirus. Norovirus. Influenza. *Staphylococcus aureus.* Candida. *E. coli* . . ."

Vinny sat on the floor and started to stretch his legs. "It won't be that bad, guys." His back made a loud *crack* and he got kind of stuck in the bending position. "Okay, it will. I agree with Hal. Let's get it over with. Let's be prepared to lose."

I sat down and leaned against my dad's duffel bag. Something rock-hard dug into my back. "Ow," I said. "Stupid flashlight."

I shoved my hand inside the bag and tried to push the flashlight out of the way. While I was digging around in my camp pack, I thought about how mad my dad was about my score.

And how much madder he was going to be after I lost the tug-of-war.

And that's what gave me the idea.

"How about this, guys? How about we don't lose the tug-of-war."

"That's pretty funny, Hal," said Vinny.

"Hear me out. Maybe all we need to win is something . . . extra."

"Extra what?"

"Extra weight. To make the teams more even. We can each take something from my duffel bag and put it inside our clothes."

I pulled the gear out of my giant bag and laid some of it on the floor.

1940s flashlight:	20 pounds
1930s canteen:	20 pounds
Shovel from Stone Age:	40 pounds
1930s chisel:	15 pounds

"That is the stupidest idea ever," Vinny said. "Even if we could carry all that stuff, how would we hide it?"

"What if we wear long pants and shirts? And put everything underneath?"

The guys just sat there and stared at me.

"Here, let me try," I said, pulling some pants and shirts out of the bottom of my pack.

The flashlight slid inside one of the pants legs pretty easily. But I had to really cram the shovel into the other leg.

"It looks lumpy," said Scot. "How are you going to bend your legs? How are you going to keep that stuff from falling out?"

"I happen to have just the thing."

I reached around in my bag until my hand

landed on something small and tight. With an elastic waistband.

Helping wimpy kids win a tug-of-war:
a job dinosaurs never expected.

"I have a whole pack of these underwear," I said. "They'll fit like the skin on a grape."

I could tell the guys were not convinced. But we had no other ideas. And it was time to go.

Doo Doo Loot!

Vinny sighed. "Okay, let's do it," he said.

The tug-of-war was going to be held in the middle of the clearing. Which wasn't too far from our cabin. But still, the trip felt pretty long.

The whole way there, I was sweating buckets because of the long sleeves and pants. Not to mention the *thirty pounds* of metal objects an inch from my kiwis.

But for the first time since we got to camp, I felt something I hadn't felt before. I think Vinny, Scot, and Perth felt it too.

Confidence.

We reached the clearing just as Theo and some of the other counselors finished spreading out the rope.

Half of it was on one side of a line. Half of it on the other.

"Whoever goes over the line first loses," said one of the counselors. He straightened out the rest of the rope, then stood to the side, next to the families and the other campers who had gathered in the clearing.

"Good luck, Hal."

I turned to see Cora standing next to me.

"I really hope you win."

CLANK!

"What was that noise?" she asked.

"Nothing."

CLANK CLANK

She looked down at my shirt and pants. "It sounded like metal . . ."

"Oh, um, that's my belt. Buckle. Yeah, it's pretty loose. Gotta go fix it. See ya!"

I walked through the crowd of kids and families and ended up right next to Mr. Prentice.

He was getting ready to announce the tug-of-war. And figure out which cabins would compete against each other.

"Hear ye. Hear ye," he said. "As many of ye know, the game tug-of-war was very special to the Jamestown settlers. Why? Well, times were tough. Tug-of-war was a way to let off steam."

He lifted one end of the rope. "The settlers played tug-of-war because they had plenty of rope from the ships. Anyone could participate. And of course, the zip line had not yet been invented."

Mr. Prentice chuckled at his joke for a good five minutes before he pulled himself together. He picked up a Pilgrim hat and held it up for everyone to see.

"Each cabin shall pick a colored piece of paper from this hat. Matching colors will compete against each other. Cabin One, please step up."

Ryan Horner stepped forward, reached into the hat, and pulled out a piece of paper.

"Green!" Mr. Prentice shouted. "Cabin two, ye shall pick next."

Mr. Prentice held the hat toward me. I reached in, grabbed a piece of the paper, and held it up for him to see.

"Green!"

"It is decided, then. Cabin One against Cabin Two. Ye shall go first!"

"But, Mr. Prentice," I said. "Ryan and Billy and their bunkmates are huge. Way huger than us. It's unfair!"

"'Tis no more unfair, Mr. Rifkind, than having to harvest nonexistent crops during a bitter cold winter." He took a step toward me. "Achhh. In these dang shoes."

Vinny, Scot, Perth, and I took our places on the rope across from Ryan, Billy, and the other two gigantors from Cabin 1.

On the sidelines, my mom was waving like crazy,

and Grampa Janson gave me two thumbs up. "Go Cabin Two!" they yelled.

Only one thing was missing from this sporting event. Good food.

Mr. Prentice lifted the gourd high in the air. "On your mark . . ."

I looked at the gourd, then turned to face Ryan, who was staring *daggers* right through me. "Where are my pearls, Cartboy?" he said. And then, before I could answer, "You are going down."

Mr. Prentice lifted the gourd higher. "Get set!"

I quickly reached in my underwear to secure the shovel and the flashlight. Then I steeled myself on the rope.

And then came Mr. Prentice's last command. "Goeth!"

Right away, Vinny, Scot, Perth, and I started pulling. And pulling. And grunting. And sweating. And clanging.

While we were pulling, the strangest thing happened: We were actually holding our own.

Ryan and Billy and their bunkmates were holding on to their side of the rope. But they weren't pulling hard. In fact, they didn't seem to be pulling at all.

What were they doing? Was Ryan going to let us win? Did he feel guilty about the desserts? Had seeing my family changed his mind about being so mean to me?

That must be it!

"Okay, guys," I said to my team. "Hang in there and pull. We have this in the bag—"

That's when I saw Ryan turn to his bunkmates, move his lips, and form one tiny little word: *"HEAVE!"*

And then, before we could do anything, another: *"HO!"*

They yanked the rope with everything they had. A second later, Scot, Perth, Vinny, and I were way up in the air. Heading straight over the line in the middle.

The funny thing is, I always wondered what it would be like to fly. And today, I got to find out. It's kind of fun. Being high in the air.

Until you crash to the ground with a rib-crushing *BONK!*

When I came to, Vinny, Scot, Perth, and I were tangled in the rope. Our pants and shirts had pretty much popped completely open.

Vinny had a chisel, a mess kit, and a flashlight on his chest. My dad's canteen conveniently landed near Scot's mouth. And a shovel ended up right on Perth's stomach.

FAARRT!

"Ha ha. Ho ho." Ryan and Billy fell on the ground, laughing.

I squinted toward the sidelines and saw Cora, Theo, and a bunch of kids staring at me. Some of them were pointing toward my pants. Which made sense. Seeing as how they had slipped down and my dinosaur underwear was in plain view for all the world to see.

Mr. Prentice came over and sized up the situation. "Sacred Saint of Skivvies," he said.

And then it was not just Ryan and Billy, but the *whole camp* laughing.

I stood up and threw my dad's old junk off me. How could I be so dumb, I thought. Why did I think his stuff would be of any use? Why would it ever help me?

"Are you okay, Hal?" My mom was standing above me, reaching out her hand.

I was just about to grab it. Then I saw my dad walking toward me with the look on his face. Yep. The same one he had when I showed him my bead-work.

Before my dad reached me, I stood up and walked straight toward the woods on the edge of camp.

I had no plan. Just two feet going in front of each other.

"Hal, wait!" I heard my mom say.

"Hal, come back!" said my dad.

But when I reached the woods, my walk turned into a run.

And I just kept on running.

Field Trip

Dear Friend from the Future:

I ran through the woods so fast, it was like my feet were attached to someone else's body.

The trees rushed by me and the sticks snapped under my feet, and all I could think was: Get away. Get away. Away from my dad and Mr. Prentice and Ryan Horner and everything.

I was running and panting and sweating. And had no idea what to do. Except keep running.

I ran until I stopped hearing people call after me. Until I stopped hearing any sounds of civilization at all.

When my feet finally stopped moving, the woods were quiet. Deadly quiet. All around me were trees, trees, and more trees. The light was fading, and the trees cast dark shadows everywhere. Darker, it seemed, every second.

I sat down on a log, and pictured how I was totally lost. How I'd never make it out of the woods alive. No one would find my body for years. And by the time they did find it, I'd have been eaten by vultures or raccoons.

Raccoon claws: designed by nature to rip the lid off a jar of Marshmallow Fluff in three seconds.

My stomach growled so loudly, a flock of birds flew out of a tree. I was *starving*. And so thirsty, my mouth felt like sandpaper.

If only I could figure out how to get back to camp.

I grabbed a stick off the ground and squinted up at the setting sun. Why? Why hadn't I listened when Mr. Prentice showed us how to make a compass using a stick and the sun's position in the sky?

I combed the forest for anything that looked like food, and spotted a patch of wild mushrooms growing near my feet.

Could I eat one? Was it safe? Would I die after it touched my lips? Mr. Prentice had talked about edible versus poisonous mushrooms during one of his lectures. But I was too busy thinking about the treasure to listen.

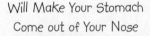

Perfectly Safe   Will Make Your Stomach
                       Come out of Your Nose

Guess which one the vultures were hoping I'd eat?

Once again, my stomach howled. Begging me to feed it.

I would have to take my chances. I lifted the mushroom to my mouth. Opened wide. And was just about to bite it—

VROOM VROOM.

I stopped because of the noise.

VROOM VROOM.

What was it? Was it a person? Did Ryan follow me?

Maybe it was a bear. The same bear that left the fur on the edge of the woods at Camp Jamestown. The night the boy went missing.

"Yaahaa." I jumped back when I saw a shadow move in the woods, but when I looked again, the shadow was gone.

VROOM VROOM VROOM.

There it was again. The noise was smooth and repetitive. Like a motor. I scanned the dark shadowy woods and realized there was only one thing to do. Follow it.

VROOM VROOM VROOM.

My feet stumbled through the forest, past a thousand pine trees and the jaws of countless woodland animals who were waiting to eat me.

Finally I came out on a small two-lane highway.

There was a car a few hundred feet away, and as it came toward me, it slowed down.

A skinny guy with long hair leaned out the window. "Hal? Hal, is that you?"

"Theo?"

"Climb in."

I opened the passenger door and jumped in so fast, I sat on his grandfather's feathered cap, which was sitting on the passenger seat.

"Sorry, Theo," I croaked.

"Hal. What happened? Are you okay? Why did you run away?"

I would have answered his questions. Except for one thing. I didn't feel like talking.

I guess Theo got the clue that I wasn't in the mood for conversation. "What do you say we ride to Colonial Williamsburg together?" he said. "We can talk about it there."

A couple of minutes later, we pulled into a restaurant.

RUNNING LIKE THE WIND
DINER

I'm pretty sure it was named after that boy who got eaten by the bear.

All the waitresses were dressed as either pioneers or Indians. The pioneers had on long skirts and bonnets, and the Indians were wearing beaded leather dresses.

A lady wearing a giant Indian headdress showed Theo and me to some seats at the counter.

We ordered cheeseburgers and salads, but getting lost in the woods must have shaken me to the bones. I could hardly look at my food, let alone eat it.

While I was staring at my burger, Theo walked to a pay phone at the far end of the diner.

"I called camp," he said when he got back. "Told them you're okay. They asked me why you ran away, but I didn't know what to say. So I told them you were playing a practical joke. You know, camp stuff."

"Thanks, Theo."

"I ran away once," he said. "After my grandfather got sick. I didn't know what to do. So I just . . . took off."

"Did you go back home?"

"Yes. Eventually. My parents were pretty mad. But in the end, they forgave me."

Theo pushed the burger in my direction.

"Why don't you eat, Hal?"

I looked down at the burger, but instead of eating, my mouth started to talk. "That's nice for you,

Theo," I heard myself say. "About your parents. But the thing is, my dad is *never* going to forgive me. I think he hates me."

"Are you sure about that?"

"Yes. I mean, first of all, history is his favorite thing in the world. And I almost failed history last year. Then he sent me to Camp Jamestown. Where I got *zero* hats."

"That doesn't mean he hates you—"

"I'm a total embarrassment to him. I might as well just keep on running."

"You're not a total embarrassment, Hal. Your leather beading was nice. And your bow-and-arrow skills were not bad. I mean, you really nailed that squirrel on the other kid's target . . ."

"I'm sure you were good at other things too, Hal."

I thought for a few seconds, then looked up at Theo. "I found a clue to the treasure," I said.

"Treasure?"

"Yeah. I'm not supposed to say anything. But I'll tell you. Seeing as how there's no way we'll find it now. The treasure is a bunch of pearls buried by Sam Prentice."

I told Theo the whole story. How Vinny told me about the treasure on the bus. How we spent the past two weeks hunting for it.

"Are you sure it's buried on camp grounds?"

"Five hundred feet west of the B. E. Whatever that is."

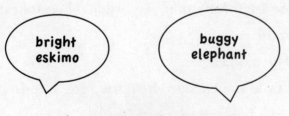

bright eskimo

buggy elephant

Theo's guesses were about as good as everyone else's.

"We thought the B. E. was the big elm. In the middle of camp," I said. "But then Vinny said he wasn't sure. And now I'm not so sure either."

"I bet you can figure it out, Hal. If you really try. Why don't you think about it while you eat your salad?"

The waitress in the Indian headdress came by and asked Theo if he wanted some coffee. "We're having a special today. Vanilla hazelnut . . ."

I watched her pour the special coffee into Theo's cup, and while I was sitting there, something flashed in my brain.

It was the word "special."

I thought about what was special to the Powhatan Indians. What my dad had told me the day before I left for camp. And what Theo told me in the museum.

The bald eagle.

Could the treasure be buried five hundred feet west of a bald eagle's nest? Not the big elm?

If that was the case, all I had to do was figure

out where the bald eagle's nest was. Or where it would have been when Sam Prentice was alive . . .

Eenie . . . meenie . . . meine . . . moe . . .

"Theo, can you drive me back to camp?"

"Yes. But not until you finish eating."

I scarfed down my cheeseburger, and it was the best thing I'd ever tasted.

Practical Jokes Played A

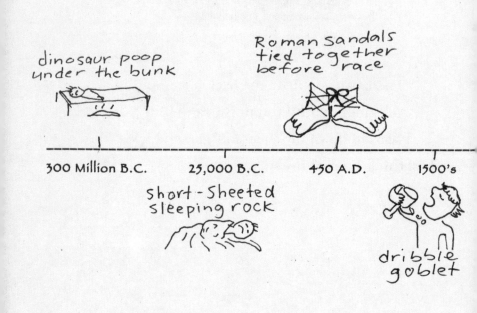

dinosaur poop
under the bunk

Roman sandals
tied together
before race

---

300 Million B.C.   25,000 B.C.   450 A.D.   1500's

Short-Sheeted
sleeping rock

dribble
goblet

Camp Through the Years

the old switcheroo

Instagram:
you making out
at camp dance

—————————————————————————————

1700's   1990   Today   Future

"customized"
camp shorts

drew mustache
on robot
counselor
while he was
sleeping

The Grand Prize

Dear Whoever You Are:

The minute Theo and I got to the camp parking lot, I jumped out of the car.

"Thanks, Theo!" I yelled when my feet hit the ground.

I had to find Vinny as fast as I could. Tell him that the B. E. might be the bald eagle. It was pretty dark out, so I figured we might get in some digging before anyone knew I was back.

I ran through the clearing and up to my cabin steps.

"Hal!"

A huge lantern shone on my face. My mom and the twins charged up to me and hugged me so hard, I practically fell on Bea and Perrie.

"Hal's back! He's back! Oh, thank God. Please don't do that again." My mom had a big tear in her eye, and Grampa Janson smiled so wide, his dentures nearly flew out of his mouth.

Everyone was falling all over me, but my dad kind of hung back. I could tell he wasn't exactly sure what to do: hug me or send me to the stockade.

How kids were punished before you could take away
TV, electronics, or Mountain Dew.

"Mr. Prentice is about to hand out the award for Best Pioneer!" said my mom. "Guess what? Your girlfriend Cora won!"

"I wouldn't say she's my girlfriend—"

"Let's all go to the bonfire." My mom grabbed the twins and started to walk toward the pond. "All the families are there."

The counselors had built a huge bonfire down by the pond, and everyone was gathered around it. My family and I took a spot in the area right next to the cattails. Or, as I like to call it, "the scene of the mosquito catastrophe."

Cora was standing near the fire, surrounded by Mr. Prentice and all the campers, families, and counselors. Everyone clapped and cheered while she held up the grand prize.

You guessed it: her very own butter churner.

"I would like to dedicate this award to my great-great-grandmother, going all the way back to the 1600s," Cora said to the crowd. "I think she would have been proud."

There was a huge round of applause while Cora's family bombarded her with hugs. I stood there, looking up at Cora, and the truth is, I felt kind of in awe of her too. Not only had she earned the grand prize, but her biceps were able to sustain the weight of an antique butter churner for two whole minutes too.

While everyone was clapping and cheering, my dad came over and touched me on the arm. I could tell it was time for "the talk."

"Son, come with me," he said.

I followed my dad a few feet away from the crowd, to a little patch of grass near a pine tree.

"What were you thinking, Hal? Running away like that. You scared the bejeezus out of your mom and me."

I wanted to answer him. But I was having a lot of trouble thinking of what to say. I looked all around me—at the camp, the cabins, the outhouses, at all the old stuff everywhere. Stuff that only a history lover would like.

I took a breath. "You want me to be you, Dad. And I can't."

"Hal, I don't want you to be me—"

"Why else would you send me here? To Camp Jamestown. You are the person who loves this place. Who loves to learn history. Not me."

"Okay, yes. I sent you here to learn history, Hal. But it wasn't just that. I wanted you to have fun too. As the historian Thucydides once said, 'History is philosophy teaching by examples.'"

"What are you saying, Dad?"

"Let me put it this way, Hal. There must be something about history you like."

I glanced around camp, at every pioneer activity, trying to find something that was fun. Something I enjoyed doing while I was here. I looked and looked, and was about to give up. But then my eyes landed on the patch of ground behind the museum.

"There was one thing," I said. "Hunting for a treasure that was buried a long time ago."

I took another look at the back of the museum, and a thought came to my mind: Maybe the whole time I had been hunting for the treasure, I wasn't just trying to get a new scooter.

Maybe I was also hunting for the pearls because I thought they had a lot of historical value. And I wanted to be a part of uncovering that.

"So, yes, Dad," I said. "I guess you could say I liked looking for the pearls."

"There you go! That's great son. Wait. Did you say pearls? What pearls?"

I was about to tell my dad about Sam Prentice and his diary, but right then, Ryan Horner walked by. He saw me talking to my dad and decided to stroll right up to both of us.

"Excuse me, Mr. Rifkind, may I have a word with your son?" he said in a big phony voice.

Ryan pulled me away from my dad, and all of a sudden his voice changed back to normal: Deep. Gravelly. And evil.

"Cartboy, you better find those pearls for me before we leave this place. Or seventh grade is going to feel like one long prison sentence."

On the upside, the food might *be better* than Camp Jamestown's.

Ryan turned around, flashed my dad a fake smile, then walked away.

"What was that about, son?" he said. "And what's all this talk about pearls?"

"Dad, I can't tell you now. I . . . I have go," I said.

I started to walk back toward the bonfire. As

I did, I heard my dad call after me. "Hal, wait. Tell me what's going on . . ."

As I kept walking, I couldn't help but think that when I got home, I was *definitely* going to be grounded for walking away from my dad again.

But I had no choice.

I had to find Vinny.

Pearls

Dear Reader:

It only took me a minute to locate Vinny. He was standing on the far side of the bonfire with Perth and Scot.

"Hey, guys," I said when I got near them.

At first, they wouldn't look me in the eyes. They pretty much pretended they didn't know me.

"So, um," I said. "I'm really sorry about everything. My score. The tug-of-war. The stupid idea to put all that stuff inside our clothes."

The guys shuffled and shifted around a lot. It

felt like about an hour, until finally Vinny said, "It's okay, Hal."

"Yeah, no worries, Hal," said Scot. "The truth is, I was pretty thirsty. That canteen came in handy."

Perth faced me and rubbed his belly. "Honestly, that shovel hit my stomach so hard, it unclogged the pipes pretty good. Haven't felt this clear in weeks."

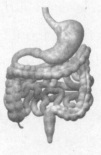

Average length of human intestine: twenty-five feet.
Average number of Double Stuf Oreos you can
fit in twenty-five feet: 153.

Scot and Perth went back to watching the bonfire. So I took the opportunity to whisper in Vinny's ear.

"I need to talk to you. I think the B. E. stands for bald eagle. Not big elm."

Vinny and I left the bonfire and walked behind a tree so nobody could hear us. I told Vinny how I got the idea when I was watching a waitress at the diner. How I remembered that the bald eagle was sacred to the Powhatan Indians.

"Even if the pearls are five hundred feet west of a bald eagle's nest," Vinny said, "how would we ever find it? There are a million trees here that could have had a bald eagle's nest at the top."

"Maybe we can figure it out."

"The bonfire is almost over. There's no time left . . ."

"I know. Let's think. Quickly. Where would a bald eagle's nest have been?"

"Well . . ."

CRUNCH CRUNCH.

"Shhh. I hear footsteps," I said. "Someone's coming."

"Shhh? Why shhh? What are you guys talking about?"

It was Cora. She walked right up to us and dropped the butter churner at my feet.

60 lb. butter churner

\+

foot

\=

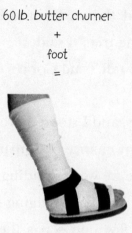

"What bald eagle nest?" she said.

Vinny and I stood there, staring at Cora, not sure of what to say.

"What nest? What are you guys talking about?"

"Maybe we should tell her, Vinny," I said. "Maybe she can help."

Vinny nodded, so I took that as a yes.

"Okay," I said. "Here's the thing. Since the day camp started, we've been looking for a buried treasure. Vinny and I found some clues. But we need to figure out where a bald eagle's nest would have been in the 1600s."

Unfortunately, Cora looked completely stumped.

"We figured the nest would have been at the top of a tall pine tree," I said.

"They're all tall," said Cora.

"True."

Cora, Vinny, and I stood there in silence. Mystified. Beyond any chance of figuring it out.

From where we were standing behind the tree, you could hear the camp singing songs around the bonfire. After a few more songs, the bonfire would be over. Our last chance to search would come to an end.

"You know what?" I said. "This is too hard. It's a needle in a haystack. A wild goose chase. A million-to-one—"

"Hold on," said Cora. "I just thought of something. When I was little, my great-grandmother was always telling me stories about the Powhatans. Stories that had been handed down for generations."

Cora looked up at the trees all around us. "There was this one story. About a bald eagle who had built a nest at the top of the tallest tree in Jamestown. Legend had it, Chief Powhatan would put gifts for the bald eagle at the bottom of the tree."

"Okay. But how can we know which tree was the tallest back in 1607?"

"My great-grandmother said the tree was next to a square-shaped rock."

"In all your digging over the years, Vinny, you didn't happen to come across a square-shaped rock, did you?" I asked.

"No. Wait. Yes! There's a square rock right outside our cabin!"

"Thanks, Cora," I said. "You saved us. We gotta go, now. We have to dig."

"Wait. I'll go with you. We'll find the pearls faster together."

I may not have become an expert pioneer at Camp Jamestown. But at least I learned something in the past two weeks:

You don't say no to Cora.

I ran inside Cabin 2, grabbed my shovel, and headed toward the door. Just before I stepped outside, I noticed something standing in the corner, by my bed.

My dad's old ax.

It was rusty. Heavy as a boulder. And as old as dirt.

But still, I grabbed it. Which if you think about it, was a pretty dumb thing to do. Why would I need an ax to dig?

There was no reason. Except that maybe I just wanted something from home.

I caught up with Vinny and Cora about five hundred feet west of the square rock. It was just past the back of the museum. Just past where we had been searching all along.

The three of us dug as fast as our arms could move.

"Hurry!" I said.

We dug to the left. We dug to the right. We dug up, down, and everywhere, but—nothing.

Even Cora looked exhausted.

We could hear the whole camp singing the last song of the night. It was a good-bye song. About how much "we're all gonna miss each other."

Chance that a song with the lyrics "gonna miss you"
was written by Taylor Swift: 93 percent.

I was so tired and mad and defeated, I slammed my shovel into the ground. "Let's just forget it," I said.

And that's when I hit something hard. So hard, my shovel made a loud *THONK*.

Cora bent over and frantically pulled away the loose dirt. There, buried a few feet underground, was an old wooden box.

"Look," said Cora. "There's a carving of Chief Powhatan on the top."

We pulled the box out of the ground and took a closer look. "It's locked!" she said. "Good thing you brought that ax."

!

The ax! I grabbed it off the ground and tried to raise it above my head. "Hnnnhhhh . . ."

"Wait, Hal. Before you open the box, there's something I want to tell you."

And then, Cora leaned in. And by that, I mean *leaned in*. Right toward my *face*. The way they always do during the mushy part of movies my mom watches on the Lifetime channel.

Things You Can Use to Cover Your Eyes
When They Kiss on TV

"*Smoochy smoochy smoochy,*" said a deep gravelly voice behind us.

I turned to face Ryan.

"I've been looking all over for you, Cartboy," he said. "Looks like you found my treasure."

Right then and there, I decided I wasn't going to back up. Or run away. Or give him what he wanted.

Instead, I was finally going to stand up to Ryan Horner.

The only problem: He was six feet tall. And I was practically a midget. He was gonna tear me apart the same way Wolfie did last fall. When Ryan and his buddies threw me in his pen.

Ryan put his puffy face right in front of mine. "So you need a girl to help you dig? What's the matter, Cartboy? Too scared out here by yourself?"

"Leave her out of this," I said.

"Oooh. Whatcha gonna do? Hit me with your rusty old ax?"

"You think you can make fun of my dad's ax?"

And then I did what any small kid with zero practical fighting experience would do.

I jumped on Ryan Horner's *back*.

Back jumping.
A famous WWE maneuver that does nothing.

Ryan tried to throw me off, but I squeezed his neck hard. "And another thing, Horner. For your information, it *wasn't me* who tattletaled on you."

"Oh, sure. Then who was it?"

"Maybe it was one of your so-called friends. Like Warren."

"Yeah, right."

"I saw him talking to Mr. Tupkin after school that day. Warren. Not me."

The truth is I was kind of guessing on the whole Warren thing. I had no idea if it was Warren, or another kid, or nobody. But something I said must have struck a chord with Ryan. Because just for a second, he loosened his grip.

"Cora, get the pearls!" I shouted.

Cora grabbed the box and started to run. Before she could get anywhere, Ryan tackled her like a *pit bull*.

I ran to Cora, but as soon as I got there, Ryan yanked the box out of her hands. He started to take off.

"Get him!" Cora said.

Cora, Vinny, and I raced after Ryan. We probably would have caught him except for three things:

He was faster.
Stronger.
And much better fed.

Ryan disappeared into the dark. While Cora and I could do nothing but stand there and watch.

What could I say?

"I guess Ryan won."

That was pretty much what I was thinking of saying, when I heard a bunch of feet pounding the ground.

"Who is it? Who's there?" I said.

And then I got the answer. It came in the form of two small kids: one wearing NightTime diapers. And another with extremely clean hands.

Scot was holding one end of a rope. And Perth was holding the other. It looked just like the rope we had used in the tug-of-war.

"Going somewhere, Ryan?" Scot said.

Sheer genius, I thought as I heard Ryan trip and fall down.

"Marco for the love of Polo! What is going on out here?"

Mr. Prentice must have heard all the commotion. Suddenly, he was standing right next to us, and the rest of camp was not far behind him.

The light from Mr. Prentice's lantern shone everywhere, and after a second, it landed on the wooden box. It had broken open, and the ground was covered with pearls.

"Who found this?" asked Mr. Prentice.

"Hal did," said Cora.

Mr. Prentice picked up a few pearls and turned them over in his hands. The way he rolled those pearls around, it was as if he wasn't just holding something old. It was like he was touching the past.

He reached out his hand, full of pearls, and put it next to mine. "Well, then, Mr. Rifkind, these are yours."

"No, they're not, sir."

I pointed to the person standing next to me. "They belong to Vinny."

Vinny hesitated a second, then took the pearls from Mr. Prentice. "Are you sure, Hal?"

"Yep."

Mr. Prentice leaned toward Vinny and spoke in a hushed and somber voice.

"Mr. Ramirez. This discovery constitutes the biggest news to hit Camp Jamestown since little Roger Edmund found Chief Powhatan's deerskin leggings."

I'm pretty sure today these are called Uggs.

"Therefore," said Mr. Prentice, "in the tradition of the settlers of Jamestown, might I propose a trade? Might ye consider donating this treasure to the museum? So that the whole world may enjoy it?"

"The whole world?" asked Vinny.

"Okay, a few dozen campers and their parents."

"Sure, Mr. Prentice," he said.

But before Vinny turned away, something weird happened. I guess you could say the pioneer in me actually came alive.

Because I couldn't help but force my way into a barter with the natives. "Mr. Prentice, as part of the trade, maybe Vinny and Scot and Perth could have one or two pearls. For themselves?"

"It's a deal!"

I guess my newfound "pioneer spirit" wasn't lost on Mr. Prentice. "Very good, Mr. Rifkind!" he said. "Trading was key to the colonists' ultimate prosperity. From the minute the British arrived in Jamestown, they began to barter with the Indians."

He took a few steps closer to me. "Now, Mr. Rifkind, the British brought something on their ship that interested the Indians very much. Can you guess what it was?"

"Um, I'm not too good at the guessing stuff, Mr. Prentice."

"Go ahead! Give it a try. During a long cold winter, what would the Indians have wanted from England? Think of something that is very British."

"Fish and chips?"

"No."

"A double-decker bus?"

"No. Something the British could have transported on their ship several centuries ago."

"The queen?"

"Mother of Crumpets! It's tea. Hal. Tea!"

But this time, when he told me the right answer, Mr. Prentice wasn't mad. He actually had a big smile on his face.

"Speaking of tea," he said, "what do you say we all go to the dining hall and have some!"

"Sounds good," I said.

I'm not the biggest tea fan in the world. But there's one thing I've learned in my short time on earth:

Where there's tea, sometimes there's also banana cream pie.

Camp Newspaper Headline

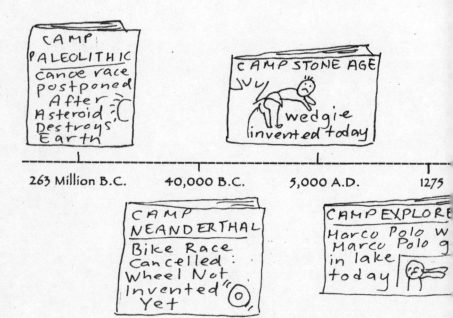

hrough The Ages

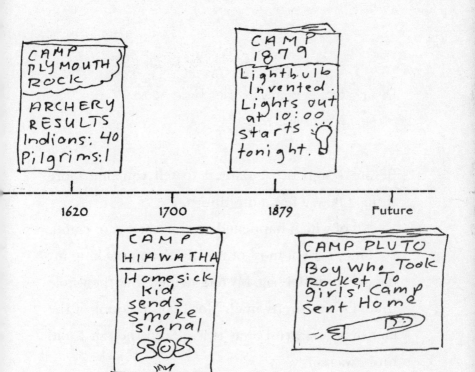

CAMP PLYMOUTH ROCK

ARCHERY RESULTS
Indians: 40
Pilgrims: 1

CAMP 1879

Lightbulb Invented. Lights out at 10:00 starts tonight.

1620   1700   1879   Future

CAMP HIAWATHA

Homesick kid sends smoke signal

SOS

CAMP PLUTO

Boy Who Took Rocket To girls' Camp Sent Home

The Dance

Dear Future Person Who Has Once Again
Allowed Me to Bug You:

Before I sign off, I wanted to tell you one more thing. Okay, a few more things.

All of which happened on the last day of camp.

First, I spent most of the afternoon packing my big green duffel bag. My dad helped, but the whole time, he was pretty mad. Mostly on account of the fact that I had run away twice. Even though I told him I was sorry.

Together we pushed the shovel to the bottom of the bag. "Am I grounded, Dad?" I asked.

"No, son. You're not."

"Oh, thank you. Oh, what a relief—"

"Except for one thing, Hal. When we get home, no *RavenCave.*"

"B-but Dad. Arnie and I have to get to Level 15! We're so close. And besides, what else are we going to do for the rest of the summer!"

"Well, son. There's a place in downtown Stowfield. It's called a library. They have these things called *books*. In fact, they have a whole section on history."

All I know is, when it comes to my dad and history, there's not much point in arguing.

"Okay," I said. "But I have one more question: Do I still have to carry my books to school in the cart next year? I mean, maybe . . . maybe I could get a motorized scooter?"

My dad took his hands off the duffel bag and

rubbed his chin. I could tell he was mulling over the whole scooter thing. Thinking about the situation. Trying to come up with an answer.

Finally, he made a decision. I was about to learn my fate.

He looked me straight in the eyes and said, "We'll see, son. We'll see."

After I finished packing, I caught up with Vinny, Scot, and Perth down by the pond.

Vinny picked up a nice flat rock and skipped it over the water.

"Seven skips!" shouted Perth. "Nice job, Vinny."

"Let me try." Scot picked up a flat rock and rubbed his hands over the smooth edges.

"No Purell today, Scot?" I asked.

"Nah. Decided I'm not gonna worry. Well, not as much. We'll see what happens when we get back on the bus with all those kids, though . . ."

Let's just hope the Purell factory is working overtime.

The pond was silvery and calm in the evening light. So I figured I'd skip a rock too. I spotted a flat, pointy one on the ground and picked it up.

Just as I was about to skip the rock across the water, I noticed it wasn't a rock. It was an arrowhead.

"You should keep that, Hal," said Vinny. "Arrowheads are supposed to bring good luck."

"I think this one already has."

"How so?"

"I heard Ryan Horner got sent home early."

Vinny turned and faced Scot, Perth, and me. "What do you say we all go to the dance together?"

"Why not?" said Perth, giving his diaper a snap. "I'm feeling pretty lucky tonight."

When we got to the entrance of the dining hall, Cora came running over.

I took the arrowhead out of my pocket and put it in her hand. "Congratulations on winning Pioneer Day," I said.

"Thanks—"

"I mean, you know. Even though your beading design was pretty inferior. To mine. Next time, you might want to try a corn dog. Or Cracker Jacks . . ."

She gave me a little punch in the arm. Which was too bad. Because when it comes to punches and Cora, you're in for a bruise the size of Kentucky.

Home of some excellent fried chicken
and college basketball.

Cora grabbed my shoulders and turned me around. "Let's go see the dining hall. We just finished decorating," she said.

We walked inside the building, and at first, I wasn't sure we were in the right place. It was nothing like the dining room where we had spent the last two weeks.

Everywhere I looked were arrowheads and artifacts and carvings. There were paintings of Powhatan men and women that looked so real, it felt like they were right there, in the room. The walls and tables were covered with pottery and jewelry. All the things Mr. Prentice's campers had found and made over the years.

One corner of the room was filled with stuff

our camp made during the past two weeks. I didn't think all our pioneer activities had added up to much. But I was wrong.

Together our camp had constructed the entire roof of a cabin. Dug two whole canoes. And beaded enough leather to make a "quilt" on the wall.

We also shot a grand total of eighty-seven animal targets. Enough to feed the entire Jamestown settlement. If the animals were real. And not made of paper. Which I hear is not very good to eat.

Calories: 35
Nutritional value: Negative 3

I didn't want to admit it, but when I saw that history stuff all over the room, my knees went a little soft. It was like we had walked into the 1600s. And it was kind of cool to be there.

I took a look around and realized there were only a few hours left of camp. Soon, I'd be back on the bus to Stowfield. Back to middle school. Back to life with my parents, my sisters, and probably, an old-lady cart full of books.

Yep. Just a few hours left to enjoy all that Camp Jamestown had to offer.

At the far end of the dining hall, Theo was standing at a turntable, wearing his grandfather's feathered cap. He put on a record, and music filled the entire room.

Well, I thought to myself, there's only one thing to do now.

Dance.

Acknowledgments

Many people helped in the creation of this book, and I would like to thank five in particular.

My editor, Susan Chang, who brilliantly and patiently helped craft this story.

Laura Dail, my agent, whose astute observations and general good cheer always steer the course.

And my family—Ian, Beau, and Charlie. I couldn't have done this book without your support and love, not to mention the joke contributions.

I'd also like to thank my friends and extended family for your generous efforts in spreading the word—from Australia and New Zealand to Europe and the United States. You've brought Cartboy into many homes, and I am so grateful to you for that! Much love and thanks.

About the Author

L. A. Campbell is the author of *Cartboy and the Time Capsule*. She grew up in Park Ridge, New Jersey, and attended the University of Colorado. She lives in New York City with her husband and two children.